ESCAPE FROM SAMSARA

Prophecy Allocation Series Book One

NICKY BLUE

This book is dedicated to my dear friend Simon Manning.
I so wish you were here to read it.

STAY TUNED

If you would like a free copy of the first chapter of book two in the Prophecy Allocation Series: 'Hot Love Inferno' I warmly invite you to join my Readers List below. (I never spam and only send out updates once a month. I simply can't be arsed to write them more often.)

nickyblue.com/inferno

Chapter One

THE NIGHTMARE

'The best ninja has no smell, leaves no name, and makes everyone wonder if he ever existed.'
(Master Tanba)

Barry Harris unhooked his back support as he reached down to pick up his secateurs. On his way up, he made that strangled grunting noise that men in their fifties tend to make. He looked at the time and grumbled, 'Three more bloody hours.'

He took off his beanie hat and used it to mop up the estuaries of sweat running from his armpits. Mrs Sharrod appeared at her back door.

'How's it going out here? Fancy a cuppa?'

'Oh, I'd love one! I've got a throat like a rusty bagpipe.'

'Have you got time to do my hedge and apple tree today too?'

Barry turned away, pretending to look for something as he gritted his teeth. 'I should think so.' *This is no life for a ninja,* he thought. *I'm a shadow warrior, I should be training for special missions and hunting down terrorists, not doing this bullshit.*

As Barry was hacking away at the hedge, he had the distinct feeling he was being watched — a ninja's highly attuned sixth sense is very rarely mistaken about these things. He looked round and couldn't see anyone but, as he continued, he realised there was a large pair of owl-like eyes staring at him from deep within the hedge.

'Who the hell are you?' asked Barry.

'I'm Terry Watkins, better known as "Terry the Hedge". Pleased to make your acquaintance, squire,' came the reply.

'I mean, what the hell are you doing in the middle of Mrs Sharrod's hedge?'

'Don't get your Alan Whickers in a twist, me ol' mucker. I'm not a real person, see. I'm an ethereal being from the other side. Basically, I'm yer all-singing, all-dancing cockney spiritual guide. I serve gardeners across the south of England and occasionally East Anglia when "Garry the Wheelbarrow" goes on the sick. Don't get me started on that muppet though. He's been mugging me off for centuries!'

'Er... right. How come you just appeared like that?'

'Whenever a gardener needs a bit of me wisdom, he cuts a hole in a hedge, and that's me cue. Bosh! You are then looking at my boat race. You got me for three minutes, then I do one.' Terry waggled his eyebrows up and down.

'But I don't have any problems,' Barry replied cautiously as he stepped back from the hedge, wondering if too many fish fingers could cause hallucinations.

'Everyone has at least one problem, and most people...put it like this: most people would kill to have just one problem.'

'Maybe so, but I can solve my own problems, thanks very much.'

'I hate to tell you this, mate, but solving your problems may take... how do I put it? A bit of lateral thinking. You may need to step outside of the conventional patterns and boundaries that normally govern your life,' said Terry, sagely.

'What, like getting self-help advice from a hedge, you mean?'

'You may not realise it yet, mate, but one day you will consider talking to me a very good idea.'

'Really? Until that day, I've got a great idea, why don't you fuck off?'

A flash of green light ricocheted through the hedge as Terry's big eyes vanished.

Mrs Sharrod reappeared holding a cup of tea and looking perplexed. 'Who are you talking to, Barry?'

'Oh, no one. I was just thinking aloud. Wonderful, a cuppa!'

'Would you like a chocolate biscuit?'

'No thanks. I just had a flare up of my irritable bowel. It's wreaking havoc in the downstairs department. My mum's told me to buy her a gas mask.'

'Sounds like my husband,' said Mrs Sharrod. 'How's your mum doing?'

'She's still getting her maudlin moments unfortunately. Been spending a lot of her time just staring out of our back window. I'm a bit worried about her, to be honest.'

'Bless her. Is she still going to those heavy metal concerts?'

'Yeah, that's her one remaining joy in life really. It was Mindy, my sister, who used to play it all the time when we were growing up. I think it's a way Mum can remember her. She went to see a band called Cradle Of Filth last month and has just bought tickets for Cannibal Corpse playing at the Brighton Dome soon. She spends most of her time hunting out obscure death metal bands on YouTube. For years, she's tried to get me into it but it tends to make me a bit anxious. I prefer country music.'

Barry shared a cramped one-bedroom flat with his eighty-two-year-old mum, Molly, above the Astral Waves Hair Salon on Portslade High Street. Portslade was a small seaside town on the south coast of England where people lived if they couldn't afford to be in the nearby city of Brighton. The proprietor of the hair salon was a delightful man by the name of Robbie Jarvis. Robbie, a 60s throwback, looked a bit like a wizard who had grown up in a septic tank: very groovy but best kept at arm's length. It was very well known in Portslade that he had a penchant for the older woman, and I do mean older woman. If you hadn't had at least one hip replaced, he simply wasn't interested.

When Barry got back from work, Molly was sat at the kitchen table listening to Napalm Death at ear-splitting volume, doing a crossword puzzle, and picking her nose. A seamless display in the art of multi-tasking.

'Konnichiwa, Mum.'

'Hello, dear. Are you still learning Japanese?'

'Yeah, I've got this app on my phone and I listen to it at work. I'm getting pretty good now.'

'Your dad would be so proud.' Molly got up and walked over to turn the music down. 'Shall I put some fish fingers on for you?'

'Thanks, Mum. I'm going out with Tom tonight to see a new ninja film.' Barry ambled into the front room and slumped on the sofa. He and his mum got on pretty well considering the cramped living conditions. Due to the lack of space, Barry was forced to sleep on a 1980s sofa-bed which was an absolute ball ache to set up, especially after a long day's gardening. He would have liked to leave it unfolded all the time but Molly didn't have anywhere else to practice her yoga in the afternoons. She had rented an OAP yoga workout DVD from the library and had been trying to master the Tree and Locust poses over the past six months. She found the advantages of thirty minutes of exercise a day were less backache, improved hip flexibility, and clearer nasal passages. The downside was that it made her fart like a baboon on a forty-eight-hour banana bender.

Every morning at 6.30 on the button, Molly woke up in a cold sweat, screaming obscenities that would make Ozzy Osbourne blush. This had been happening since New Year's Eve 1993, when she had seen an episode of Emmerdale where a plane had crashed into the village of Beckindale, killing four of Molly's favourite characters. Life had become devoid of value from that point onwards. Incidentally, it was also the same day her husband and daughter had nipped out for a pint of milk and never returned.

Molly came into the front room with Barry's fish fingers and sat down next to him.

'Do you know what day it is today, Barry?'

'No.'

'It would have been your dad's seventy-sixth birthday. It's twenty-five years since they went missing, but feels like forever.'

Barry put his arm around his mum and pulled her towards him.

'I know, Mum. I think about them all the time.'

'The first time I laid eyes on your father it was love at first sight. I'd never even met a Japanese person before but I knew I had to be with him.'

'Why did Dad come to England?'

'He said he was sightseeing.'

'How come he was in Portslade then?'

The police investigation into the disappearance of Mindy and Yamochi Harris found a picture of a Japanese glamour model amongst his possessions. The police believed the most likely scenario was that he had eloped with her and taken his daughter with him. The case was closed but something never sat right about it for Barry. Even the most plausible and rational of explanations can turn out to be wrong. Secretly, part of Barry blamed himself for his dad's disappearance. He felt there must be something wrong with him that had caused his dad to leave.

Barry always tried his best, but he did not really have the emotional resilience to cope with being around his mum when she was in one of her moods. He feared they might be contagious in some way, and that he might catch some kind of an emotional or mental meltdown. This was one of the reasons he spent his weekends up at his allotment. It was the only time he felt free, undisturbed by the pressures of everyday life, unaffected by the stupidity of other human beings.

Barry had had quite a difficult relationship with his sister Mindy when they were growing up. As the self-proclaimed black sheep of the family, she had left home at sixteen in a fit of dramatic hormonal rage. To announce her newfound independence she had the words "Born Free" tattooed on her neck. Her dream was to start a death metal band and tour the world. She was always highly critical of the fact that Barry had been a loner, and would often pretend they weren't related if they were seen in public together. This had confused and upset Barry deeply for years. He did, however, take some solace from the fact that she had never got a band together, and ended up on the checkout at Pound-Universe, selling cheap novelty crap to apathetic teenagers.

Yamochi began teaching Barry the sacred art of ninjutsu on his sixth birthday. At the time, Barry thought this was because he was being bullied at school, but his father would always tell him he had a much higher purpose in life that one day he would come to realise.

From that moment on, Barry had tried to model himself on the archetype of an elite ninja warrior. Mysterious, sleek, dressed in a black kimono, gracefully moving in the shadows, like a cat waiting to pounce.

There were, however, a few minor physical incongruities that Barry had to work with. For example, Barry's left leg was one inch shorter than his right. When he was having a good day he liked to joke that if he didn't lean at a twenty-three degree angle to his right, he would be walking in circles. It was not a very good joke and he didn't tell it very often. He managed to address this height discrepancy with a robust pair of custom-made Cuban-heeled boots. There was also the fact that Barry weighed sixteen stone. Apart from these very minor details, Barry was the absolute doppelganger of a badass ninja.

One of the benefits of living above a hairdresser's was that you got twenty percent off on Wednesday mornings before eleven.

'Why don't you get a long plaited ponytail extension like they have in the martial arts films, Barry?' Robbie's eyes sparkled with creativity.

'I haven't got enough hair for that, have I?'

'Don't you worry about that. They don't call me the wizard for nothing. I'll weave it into your squirrel and do a bit of backcombing. It will look totally natural.'

'Cool.' Barry sat back, picturing the transformation about to unfold.

Robbie scratched his flaky chin through his wiry goatee beard and bent down to whisper in Barry's ear. 'Here, you know your mum's mate Merril? She came over last night. We were going at it till four. I could hardly get out of bed this morning.'

'She's eighty-four, you animal!'

'Easy, tiger. I don't dig the numbers game. I can't help it if a purple rinse drives me wild. Doing the job I do doesn't help. I'm in hog heaven.'

Barry's best and only friend was a man called Tom Carter, a retired Australian gentleman who had a big cosy ginger beard and demonic halitosis. Barry had met him at the annual Ninja Film Festival in 1994. They could spend hours waxing lyrical on every aspect of ninjutsu. I say 'could' as Barry had to virtually hold his breath to have a conversation with him. On this occasion, they had met up to see *Ninja Hell Inferno Apocalypse 4* and had ended up down the pub afterwards for some crucial post-flick analysis.

Tom sat down and put his pint of cider in front of him. 'I can't believe there were only three other people in there tonight. I think most people are scared of seeing ninja unleashing their raw power like that.'

'Too right,' said Barry. 'My dad told me what the big ninja battles used to be like and it was just like in that movie. No other martial art comes close to ninjutsu – it blows them all out of the water.'

'I hear what you're saying but some of the other martial arts can be tasty too. What about kickboxing? That can be deadly. What would you do if two guys trained in that came running at you?'

'Easy. I'd jump up, and hang in mid air in the praying mantis pose so they couldn't kick me. When they got close enough I'd kick them in the teeth.'

'Sounds like something out of The Matrix.' Tom supped on his cider. 'What about if three guys trained in kung fu came at you with axes and whip chains?'

'No bother, I'd take two out straight away with ninja stars between the eyes. Then I'd read the mind of the last one and work out exactly what he was going to do and prevent every move he came up with. After a while, he would work out I was psychic, shit himself, and run away.'

'Okay, right... So what if ten guys trained in jujitsu with swords and axes trapped you in a lift?'

'Piece of piss. I'd turn myself invisible, kneel on the floor and let them slice each other to bits. When they were all dead, I'd stand up, wipe all the body parts off me, and then press the button for the floor I wanted.'

'You've got it worked out then. It's a shame that all the ninjas were wiped out by the samurai isn't it,' replied Tom, opening a packet of cheese Wotsits.

'Allegedly, but how does anyone really know? The very hallmark of a ninja is invisibility. They are off-grid stealth warriors dancing in and out of the shadows, teaching their skills to the chosen few. Like my dad teaching me, for instance.'

'But how do you know he definitely knew the ninja arts – he could have just learned it from a book?'

'No way, he was the real deal. Authenticity is not something you can pretend to have.'

Tom looked deeply into his pint of cider, as if trying to get his head around what that was supposed to mean.

'Some of his skills were incredible. He told me he could see into the past and future, and even change the shape of reality itself if he wanted to.'

'But you're not really a ninja, are you?' Tom leant in close to Barry to make eye contact, in a bid for an honest response.

'Of course I am. My dad trained me for years.' Barry slowly recoiled as his eyes started watering.

'Can you shape change?'

'I haven't tried yet.'

'Can you read minds then?'

'I'm still working on that.' Barry fiddled with his ponytail. 'I've been meditating more lately though so I think I'll get there soon.'

'Can you make yourself invisible?'

'All right, smart arse. Being a ninja isn't all like it is in the movies you know.'

'You just said it was!'

The longer life went on for Barry the more he felt frustrated by it. He often had the sense that he was losing control over his own destiny. He felt separate from other people, believing he knew a way out of this confusing mess through spiritual practice. Inspired by the ninja tradition, Barry had been ordained as a Buddhist on his fortieth birthday; something he found tricky explaining to the people surrounding him. On his way home from the pub he bumped into Merril in the bus queue, and with two pints of lager inside him, thought he'd give it a go.

'As a Buddhist, I practice the art of mindfulness.'

'Ooh what's that?' asked Merril as her bulbous green eyes became animated beneath an unkempt stringy woollen monobrow.

'By observing our feelings and sensations, we can gain insight into true reality.'

'Ooh that's sounds good, Doctor Harper gave me a relaxation tape once to help me sleep but the bleedin' seagulls outside my window were doing my nut in. I couldn't concentrate for toffee.'

'It's not easy, Merril, that's for sure, but if we carry on without any kind of self-reflection, we will never escape the Wheel of Samsara.'

'What's that, dear?'

Barry paused dramatically to show the importance of what he was about to share. 'It is... the endless merry-go-round of birth and death for all eternity. Meditation is the way we step off it. My dad used to say that with patience and compassion, meditation gets easier over time.'

'I ended up throwing a bucket full of piss over the buggers. It worked wonders; they never came back. I sleep like a baby now.'

When Barry got home, Molly had already gone to bed. Barry laid back on his futon, closed his eyes and was instantly dragged back into the terrifying recurring nightmare he had been having ever since his dad disappeared.

Barry was hanging from a ledge on the side of a steep cliff. However hard he tried, he couldn't find a foothold. Crawling along the top of the ledge were samurai warriors about to swing down their swords. If Barry let go, he would fall five hundred metres onto an outcrop of rocks below, around which a furious ocean broiled and spat. Swinging from the ledge, struggling and clinging to life, he heard the voice of his father.

'Beware the samurai ghosts, Barry. They are coming to get you!'

Barry started awake, shivering and fighting for breath. He sprang up and called out, 'Dad, where are you?'

The words echoed into the hollow darkness, the bitter strangle of two alien worlds colliding. Barry fell back onto the bed, defeated again, realising this was just another nightmare.

Chapter Two

SUSPICIOUS MINDS

L ike any self-respecting gardening ninja, Barry lived by a strict, and, he would suggest, sacred code of ethics. This wasn't a code that applied to Barry as such but rather a set of rules on how other people should conduct themselves around him. The only problem was that you weren't aware of these codes until you fell foul of them. Barry would say they should be obvious. See what you think:

- One should never besmirch the ninja philosophy.
- We should only ever focus on the beauty of life.
- Only speak if you can improve on the silence.
- Be kind to all living beings.
- Never let the enemy have your weapon.
- Don't take any shit from idiots.

A concise and consistent set of principles, I'm sure you will agree. Barry was somewhat foggy around what form of punishment any transgression should incur. Suffice to say, when Barry got angry, he was not someone you would celebrate for his forbearance.

He managed to keep a lid on his frustration most of the time. It only really spiralled out of control when he felt misunderstood, when he was being clear with people and they still didn't get him. In its most extreme expression this could give birth to an unquenchable rage, a fury that was often accompanied by an awkward tic just above the right corner of his lip. To the uninitiated, it could appear like he was attempting an Elvis impersonation. To the initiated it was time to leave the building.

There was a recent incident at Portslade library. Barry had gone in to find a book on Japanese art. He had somehow managed to set off the alarm monitors as he entered the front door.

Stanley Tilbury, the seventy-four-year-old security guard who spent most of the day chewing gum and scratching his arse, was on his feet and in Barry's face like a rat up a drainpipe. Stanley was wound up tighter than a celebrity facelift and simply born for moments like this. 'Hey punk! Smuggling a book out of the library, are we?'

'No,' replied Barry, 'I'm actually coming into the library to find a book. Who are you? Dirty Harry?'

'Don't back chat me, sunny jim, I spent thirty years in the navy! Let me look in your bag and see what you've half-inched,' barked Stan. 'You must have nicked something or why would the zinger have gone off?'

'I've got no books in my bag,' growled Barry as his lip quivered.

'Don't you raise your voice at me, you grubby little scroat! You are a thief!' Stanley grabbed at Barry's bag causing his nunchucks to come flying out and ricochet off the side of the returns counter. Stanley saw the weapon and screamed, 'Terrorist! Call the police!' He then ran bravely off in the direction of his office to raise the alarm.

Falling into a panic, Barry picked up his nunchucks and decided the only logical thing to do was to explain to everyone in the library what was happening.

'Please calm down, and listen to me. What has happened here is that the security guard has accused me of stealing, grabbed my bag and my nunchucks have fallen out. It's really nothing to worry about; the nunchucks are essentially a defensive weapon. If you had an enemy coming at you holding a sword the nunchucks can be used to trap the blade with the chain between the two sticks. Admittedly, ninjas have been known to strangle an opponent by twisting the metal chain tightly round the neck of an opponent which can actually cause a person's eyes to pop out of their skull, but that's a very rare occurrence. For those of you still looking a bit worried, I'm guessing you may have seen Bruce Lee's *Fist of Fury* where the master beats the living shit out of a gang of nunchuck-wielding students who had pissed him off. I think I know how he feels but I want to reassure you all that a ninja would never kill anyone with nunchucks. He would probably do it with his bare hands.'

Taking a deep breath, Barry realised by looking at the sea of ashen faces that his speech didn't seem to be helping with the tension levels all that much. A soft voice drifted from the back of the room, 'I'm sorry to have to say this but I can't help thinking they do look like a weapon.'

'They are not a bloody weapon!' howled Barry. 'You want see a weapon? I'll show you a weapon!' And with that, Barry went into his bag and pulled out two mini ninja swords. 'Now these are weapons! You could gut a mackerel in mid-air with these!'

An array of yelps and whimpers from the back of the library indicated that anxiety levels in the room were now reaching DEFCON 1 status. This seemed to barely register with Barry, however, and the more he felt he was losing his audience the more agitated and annoyed he became.

Mavis Greenrod, the head librarian, put her hand up. 'Can I go to the toilet please?'

'No! I'm trying to explain something to you. Sit down!' Barry's lip was in maximum Elvis mode as he continued. 'This is about Stanley, isn't it? You're all taking his side over mine, aren't you? Let me tell you a few home truths about Stanley. He's just a jobs-worth who believes he has some power. Ha!' Barry turned to project his voice towards the office, 'Here's a news flash, Stanley; you are just a little corporate puppet being played by some middle manager who probably doesn't even know your name.'

Returning to his audience, Barry continued, 'God forbid he had any real power he'd be the next Pol Pot of Portslade! He would line all of you up in the reference section and get his death squads to fill you with lead! How does that sound?'

'Stanley's really nice to me,' came a timid voice from the back of the room. 'He brings in cream buns for everyone on Fridays.'

'Ha, yes, and Hitler banned vivisection but what does that prove?' snapped Barry. 'If I were God, I'd give Stanley mood-related anal incontinence. That way every time he acted like a fascist he'd shit himself.'

'I'm going to shit myself if you don't let me go to the toilet,' replied Mavis.

Meanwhile, Stanley had decided, in the interests of national security, to set off the fire alarms and then made for the roof to signal for help. Barry chased after him in hot pursuit.

By the time the police arrived, Stanley had locked himself in the cleaning cupboard and Barry was reading the Human Rights Act to him through the keyhole.

This unfortunate misunderstanding caused a modicum of disquietude at the Harris residence later that evening.

'I will never be able to step foot in that library again you dick head,' said Molly, throwing a tea towel across the room.

'It's not my fault, Mum. That security guard is an idiot and Doctor Harper said I have "Perpetual Rage Syndrome".'

'What the hell is that when it's at home?'

'It's what happens when I get angry. I get a severe anxiety reaction that releases a huge adrenaline surge making me even more angry, and before I know it, I'm in a self-propelling anxiety rage loop which I can't get out of. It's been happening ever since Dad left.'

'I haven't got a clue what you just said but you're going back to see Doctor Harper, or I'll show you the true fucking meaning of the word anger. Get him to give you some pills to calm you down.'

Barry took the following morning off work and arrived early for his appointment at the doctor's. He was greeted with the customary 'Welcome, Mr Harris. The doctor will be with you shortly.' Barry wondered why they still spun that tired old yarn when there was always at least a sixty-minute wait.

Sitting down in the cramped and brightly lit waiting room, Barry's irritation levels rose immediately when two small children started fighting in front of him. *Why aren't the parents controlling these brats?* Barry tried to distract himself by reading the only magazine available, Celebrity Gossip, but the man opposite him was sneezing wildly in all directions.

As Barry's heartbeat accelerated, he rubbed his muculent palms down his jeans and leant back against the wall, inhaling the stagnant air. The sole topic of conversation from the elderly woman beside him rabbiting on like a well-meaning machine gun was how painful it was having your varicose veins removed.

A category ten panic attack was about to ensue when Barry heard his salvation in the words, 'Mr Harris, the doctor will see you now.'

Barry stepped inside the doorway and was hit with the unique and overwhelming scent that filled Doctor Harper's consultation room. A perfumer may have placed the fragrance somewhere between bizarre e-pipe essence and acrid body odour. It was so strong an aroma it attacked the back of your throat every time you opened your mouth. This had the effect of giving every first word of your sentence a muffled resonance. It also led Doctor Harper to wrongly diagnose a large proportion of his patients with throat infections.

Doctor Harper looked up from his case files.

'Ah, Barry, fantastic to see you! I hear you've been having a few troubles again.'

'Yes, doctor,' replied Barry sheepishly.

'The buggers have been pressing your buttons again, haven't they?'

'Yes, doctor,' Barry looked awkwardly at the floor.

'The Fucking Bastards!' bleated Doctor Harper as a long thread of drool made its way down the underside of his pipe. 'Nonetheless, you really must rein it in, boy. Take control of yourself or all hell will break loose! There's already enough madness out there! From what I read in the papers, things are getting out of control in the sexual arena. If you follow me, Barry?'

'Sorry?' Barry's cheeks began to radiate.

'Horizontal refreshment,' barked Doctor Harper with a deranged glint in his eye. 'They're all at it! If only I were single again I'd be rutting like a billy goat in mating season.' By now a small puddle of drool had collected on the desk under the drip line of Doctor Harper's pipe. Barry wriggled uncomfortably in his chair and was about to speak when Doctor Harper, warming to his subject, began again.

'I do hope I'm not being too personal, but I got married before the sexual revolution, you see. My wife, Mrs Harper, only lets me once a month and a man has his needs. Don't get me wrong, Barry, I love my wife but I see these young ladies around covered in tattoos and I get the distinct impression I'm missing out. I bet you're sticking it everywhere, aren't you? A young buck like you.'

'Er...' spluttered Barry. 'I'm single at the moment.'

'I bet you are! Very wise. One in every port, hey? I've tried to get more adventurous with her, I really have, but she's just not that way inclined. I suppose I shouldn't complain; we did try a bit of back door fun as a treat on my birthday last year, but I fear it's not enough. I have a deep itch, Barry, and it needs to be scratched.'

Barry was sweating like Big Daddy in a sauna. He was gripping the edge of his seat so tightly his knuckles had turned white, and a steam train of thoughts was hurtling through his head. *Why is he telling me these things? What am I supposed to say?*

In a bid to get the conversation on track Barry said, 'Doctor, my mum was hoping you may be able to give me some pills to stop my angry outbursts from happening again.'

'No, you don't want that. I'm going to refer you to see a very good psychotherapist I know called Doctor Thomas Gilpgünter. I think he may be able to help you.'

'Thank you Doctor. There was something else I wanted to talk to you about,' said Barry. 'It's a bit embarrassing. My IBS has been really playing me up lately, I've been finding it really hard to stick to the diet. The thing is sometimes at work if I bend over too quickly I get a bit of....How do I put it? accidental leakage. I find it all a bit distressing really.'

'That's nothing to be ashamed of Barry, I can prescribe

you some fitted underwear to wear for when you are moving around a lot, they have built in leakage pads you can swap over.'

'I'm not wearing incontinence pants Doctor, you can shoot me before that happens.'

'There's no need to think about them like that Barry, they are merely support briefs, you only need to wear them until your diet is back under control. Are you still eating all those fish fingers? You need to cut them out.'

'I am trying Doctor.'

'Look, they are very discreet, no one will ever know. Let me write you a prescription.'

Barry reluctantly took the piece of paper and after another hour of detailed accounts regarding Mrs Harper's bedroom affairs, Barry managed to abscond from the surgery. He couldn't help wondering if the entire experience had all been some huge ruse to trick him into to therapy.

When Barry got home, Molly had some fish fingers waiting for him on the kitchen table, the best kind of sedative available. It was Sunday night too, which was movie night if they could agree on something. The choices were a Metallica documentary called *Some Kind of Monster* that Molly had been itching to see for months, or *The Crying Game*.

Barry narrowly escaped a heavy metal melt down by whipping out a bumper bag of Humbugs, a ploy that was as transparent as it was successful.

They settled down on the futon with steaming mugs of hot chocolate.

'I didn't see that coming!' said Molly as the credits rolled.

'Who would have thought she'd have a pair of bollocks! I feel a little bit sad now.'

'It's just a film,' replied Barry.

'It makes me feel like a dog who's been promised a walk by its owner who then forgets and goes out. Or like the rabid whore of Babylon puking over the rotting corpse of human civilization.'

'I think I need to go to bed now, Mum.'

'Yes, alright dear.' Said Molly picking herself up. 'Sleep well.'

Chapter Three

LITTLE TIMMY AND MISS MIGGLES

L ife as a gardener is quite random. Apart from your regular clients you never quite know when or where your next job is coming from. When an inquiry came in from one of the richer postcodes of Brighton, Barry often had mixed feelings. He could charge thirty to forty percent more than his usual rate. Paradoxically however, gardening for rich people generally made him feel like a peasant worker.

It was a sunny Friday morning in July when Barry turned up to a new job in Hove. Hove is a small seaside town on the south coast of England where people move to if they have too much money to live in the neighbouring city of Brighton. The first thing Barry noticed about the house was a crucifix welded onto the large wrought iron front gates. Below the crucifix was a plaque inscribed with the legend: *If God brought you to it He will bring you through it.*

Barry whispered to himself as he opened the gate, 'good luck, mate.'

He was greeted by the lady of the house, Mrs Gann, and her very well dressed son Little Timmy.

'Good morning!' said Mrs Gann. 'I'm very pleased to see you are punctual! I like that in a man. Say hello, Timmy.'

'Hello, sir. I am very pleased to make your acquaintance.'

'What a polite young man,' replied Barry. 'You don't often get much respect for your elders these days!'

'We take great pride in good manners in this house, don't we, Little Timmy?'

'Yes, Mummy, good manners don't cost anything. Would you like to meet my cat Miss Miggles when she wakes up from her morning nap, sir?'

'That would be very nice, thank you.' Barry put down his tool bag.

Mrs Gann collected rare sea sponges for a hobby, no one in the family knew why. Little Timmy suspected it may have had something to do with his mother's debilitating piles but this was not a topic of conversation one could have in polite society. Mrs Gann had been trying to heal her haemorrhoids with raw food smoothies which seemed to be helping but she was under quite a bit of stress. Truth be told, she found it very difficult looking after Little Timmy alone although she would never have admitted that.

The reason for her lack of support was that her husband Mr Charles Gann lived in the attic in a dress. Four years earlier, Charles had come home from his job as the CEO of a large corporation and declared over dinner that he wanted a sex change. Mrs Gann understandably almost spat her teeth out. Keeping up the facade of respectability, no matter what, was of vital importance to her, and so a compromise was found. Charles would be allowed to have his sex change as long as he moved up into the attic and promised to never leave the house in daylight hours. Charles promptly changed his name to Melanie and disappeared up into the loft hatch. From that moment on, he was forced into leading the life of a transsexual vampire, sleeping on an old camping bed in the attic. Segregated from his family and work colleagues, his only crumbs of social contact were in the late night seedy drag bars he frequented. He lived on microwave meals and endless reruns of *Breaking Bad* at four a.m. He had never been happier.

Mrs Gann taught Christian Mindfulness classes for a living, which she strongly believed was a panacea for all the world's ills. Barry had only ever heard of Mindfulness in relation to Buddhism and the martial arts. This led him to the perfectly reasonable question, 'What's the difference between Christian and Buddhist Mindfulness?'

'Ah, I'm glad you asked me,' replied Mrs Gann. 'When you practice Christian Mindfulness your heart will open to the love of Christ and you find eternal salvation. When you practice Buddhist mindfulness you will be damned to suffering in hell for all eternity.'

'That's good to know,' replied Barry. 'Shall we look at the garden now?'

Being shown around a garden by a new client for the first time was always a bit of a tense affair. This was due to the fact there was normally an expectation that Barry would be able to identify and wax lyrical about the unique cultivars on display in their precious and most prized of gardens. The problem Barry had was that he didn't really like plants, in fact he found them pretty dull. This could be seen as a bit of a handicap for a gardener, but he had got away with it through most of his career with a simple game he'd invented called "botanical bluff". At horticultural college, he had memorized the Latin names of two of the world's largest plant families. So when Barry was asked to identify a rare plant in someone's garden he would always reply, 'I'm pretty sure it belongs to either the Asteraceae or the Fabaceae plant family.'

Given that the sum of plants within these two families

weighed in at forty-four thousand, Barry was quite often correct, if somewhat unspecific.

'Please pull up the ivy growing in the flower borders, but whatever you do, leave it alone on the fence,' proceeded Mrs Gann, 'That fence desperately needs to be replaced and I fear its only that blessed vine keeping it standing. We are lucky enough to have the vicar of our parish living next door, and his wife is a very keen horticulturalist. There's nothing she doesn't know about native roses and she has won East Sussex County Parish Gardener competition five years running.'

'Doesn't the vicar judge that?' asked Barry.

Mrs Gann ignored the question. 'Have you found the love of Jesus Christ in *your* heart, Barry?

'Not yet,' Barry mumbled.

'We will just have to see if we can fix that, won't we?' And with that, Mrs Gann trotted off up the path to the house.

Barry picked up his trowel, wondering how that could be 'fixed'? He had read the ontological arguments for intelligent design which he had found quite compelling. From his perspective, though, it seemed as if the entire universe had been designed to maximize his stress levels. Using this as the premise for any causal proof of God, one could only surmise that if a prime mover did exist, he very probably had a stick up his bum.

Barry had just knelt down to start weeding when he heard a rustling behind him. He turned round and saw Little Timmy staring up at him. Barry smiled.

'Hello, Timmy, has Miss Miggles woken up from her nap?'

Little Timmy stared blankly at Barry for a few moments before belting out, 'Listen, you grotty little slave, ignore what my mother just told you and go and weed Miss Miggles' shit pit over there. She hasn't been able to have a decent poo in days due to all the nettles stinging her ring piece.' As Timmy turned and marched off toward the house he shouted, 'I'll be watching you from my bedroom, so put your fucking back into it!'

Kneeling on the grass, in a mild state of confusion, Barry wasn't quite sure if that had actually happened. Maybe he had imagined it? He collected himself and then leant forward to tug away at the stubborn vine again.

Just as he was finding his rhythm, he became aware of a barely audible female voice from behind the fence. 'What's eating my beans?'

Barry pretended not to hear and went about his weeding.

The voice repeated, 'What's eating my beans?'

'Are you talking to me?' Barry stared at the fence.

'Yes,' came back the voice. 'You're a gardener, aren't you?'

'Yes.'

'I'll start again, shall I? What's eating my beans? It's not slugs as I've drowned all of them. How about woodlice or birds? Can woodlice climb up beanpoles?'

'I don't know.'

'I need an answer for this today!' came the voice, which was now clearly audible. 'So what is it? Birds or woodlice?'

' Birds... I think,' Barry spluttered.

'Good. I'll net them. That'll keep the blighters out.' The voice tailed off as the mystery woman wandered off, mumbling to herself.

Barry inhaled as he returned to the ivy and then lost himself to rumination. *Who the hell talks to someone through a fence without even introducing themselves? Must have been the vicar's wife, I suppose. Who the hell would choose this bizarre job for themselves?*

Some of the misconceptions people have prior to taking up a career as a gardener are:

− You get to spend lots of time on your own, communing with nature.

− Your body tunes in to the rhythmic and seasonal flow of life.

− You get to work at your own pace.

− You mainly plant flowers and pick strawberries all day long.

− Gardening is good for your mental health.

Barry would strongly advise you to spend a week working alongside a gardener before making any final career decision. After being covered in dog shit, ripped to shreds by rusty barbed wire, and made to pay two hundred pounds for cutting through a broadband cable (conveniently running through the middle of a hedge), you may want to realign your assumptions.

The ivy clearance was progressing quite well until Barry looked up and saw Little Timmy hanging out of his bedroom window.

'Oi, baldy, hurry up! Miss Miggles' got a turtlehead! Don't make me come down there!'

Barry's lip was firmly entering the pre-quiver phase. 'I've left my gloves at home so I can't pull those nettles up. I've been clearing the ivy out of the border like your mother asked me to!'

'Don't do that, you simpleton, what are the wood pigeons supposed to eat? A Big Mac? Miss Miggles loves chasing the wood pigeons! Any gardener worth his salt would know that.'

Darth Vader would have been proud of the glare Barry aimed at Little Timmy. *Okay, keep calm, remember what the doctor told you... Just keep a lid on it... The little bastard! Shit, what would a Buddhist do? Chant... Yes... do that.*

'May all beings be happy, may all beings be well, may—' Alas, it was all too little, all too late, for a glorious rage had descended. Barry tore nettles out of the ground with his bare hands.

In no time, they were red raw but he felt no pain. Hell hath no fury like a gardener scorned.

Little Timmy came running out of the back door of the house.

'I have just been speaking with mother about the horrendous job you are doing, and she's quite simply beside herself with stress and it's all your fault! What are you going to do about it, you lopsided midget?'

A look of terror was plastered over Mrs Gann's face as she came out to find what all the fuss was about.

'For goodness sake, keep your voices down. The vicar's wife might be in her garden. Can someone please explain what's going on here?'

'Mummy, this terrible man told me he wanted to play with your tits. I was telling him off for being so rude.'

'How dare you!' spat Mrs Gann as she turned to Barry. 'I knew you were trouble when I first laid eyes on you.'

'What!' howled Barry. 'Your son is a liar and a lunatic. I think he has serious psychological issues.'

'There's absolutely nothing wrong with my son. Unlike you, pervert!'

'You don't scare me,' said Little Timmy squaring up to Barry in a misguided attempt to intimidate him. 'You'd better get this mess sorted out or I'll go upstairs and wake up Daddy.'

On any other day, Melanie would have been deep in la la land at 11 am. Today, however, she had not long got back from a nightclub and was crashed out on top of her bed in a rather slinky lace mini skirt. She was torn from her slumber by her wife's shouting, and knew instantly it had to be an emergency, as her wife had never before been heard creating a scene, God forbid! She went flying down stairs to join the garden uprising.

On seeing her husband, Mrs Gann implored, 'What the hell are you doing, Charles? The vicar's wife might see you!'

'Sorry, darling, but I heard the commotion and had to break protocol.'

'This revolting man has been making sexual advances towards me.' Mrs Gann pointed at Barry.

'Oh really, is that the case? I suppose you will do the same with me too, will you?'

'I'd prefer you to your wife if I was forced to make a choice.'

'How dare you!' snapped Mrs Gann.

Amongst the chaos, Miss Miggles appeared from her morning nap and decided to scramble up the ivy and balance precariously on top of the wonky fence.

'You know what your problem is, don't you?' said Timmy addressing Barry. 'You're anally retentive. I know all about it from a book my mum has. Every time you have a poo you probably cry and touch your willy. If you have one.'

'That's it!' Barry detonated with a primal fury even the Hulk couldn't have mustered. He sprang to his feet and lurched towards his little tormentor. Timmy turned to run but tripped on Barry's tool bag and landed face-first into Miss Miggles' shit pit.

'Keep your hands off my son!' howled Mrs Gann.

Clambering back to his feet, his face smothered in cat excrement, Timmy looked over at Miss Miggles as she issued a cry for help. She had slipped from the top of the fence and was hanging by a solitary paw. Timmy ran blind in the direction of the distress call.

'Don't worry, I'm coming to rescue you.' Timmy ran face-first into the fence, sending it crashing down with a momentous thud into the vicar's garden. Spending one of her nine lives, Miss Miggles landed safely on the beanpoles as the vicar and his wife were revealed sitting in the garden drinking tea from their finest china. A photographer from the *Hove Parish Newsletter* was with them for an article on the recent plague of rose thrip tearing its way through the parish gardens. The startled vicar turned round just at the moment Barry decided it was prudent to rugby tackle Melanie, dragging her mini skirt down to her ankles to reveal a rather becoming set of red lacy knickers and suspenders.

The vicar supped on his tea and blithely called over, 'Afternoon, everyone! Long time no see, Charlie.'

'My name is Melanie now, vicar,' replied Melanie, trying to keep her balance.

'Shut up, Charles,' hissed Mrs Gann through gritted teeth.

The vicar turned to the reporter. 'Old Charlie over there used to be one of my finest choirboys. Funny how times change, isn't it? Why don't you get a photo for the alumni section of the newsletter?'

The photographer snapped away enthusiastically as Mrs Gann was busy trying to pull her husband's mini skirt up at the same time as prying Barry's iron grip from around his legs.

'For God's sake, can you both just please stop! This is going to ruin me!' pleaded Mrs Gann.

Little Timmy, the gift of sight restored, ran up behind Barry and kicked him hard in the anus before running off into the house.

Incensed, Barry let go of Melanie and took off after Timmy.

Barry ran into the kitchen and found himself staring at Little Timmy, who was levitating two metres off the floor in front of him. His eyes were darker than coffin trenches, his body the colour of death. One arm pointed at Barry and the other held Miss Miggles.

A shiver like cold mercury swept along Barry's spine. 'What the—'

'Eigo no hito ni shi, Eigo no hito ni shi! 'Timmy chanted Japanese in a coarse, sinister monotone, over and over like an automaton gone wrong. Barry lurched backwards in shock. He wasn't great at Japanese but he knew what it meant: 'Death to the English man'. Miss Miggles had grown ten-inch claws and steel vampire fangs. Timmy held her as high as he could, then threw her screeching at Barry. The demonic cat hurtled towards him; with only a second to act, he caught her around the neck and used a ninja head flip technique to throw her back across the kitchen. Miss Miggles let out a guttural growl, flailing through the air and landing neatly in Mrs Gann's blender. Without thinking, Barry ran over and flicked the 'on' switch. Miss Miggles would not be getting her butt stung by a nettle ever again. Barry turned as Little Timmy faded away in front of him, his chant still echoing from the bleak marble tiled walls.

As Barry made a swift exit through the rear garden gate, he remembered the day his father taught him that move, a perfectly still autumn day in Portslade park. He was fairly sure it wasn't intended for fiendish felines. It did occur to him, however, that a Miss Miggles smoothie might be just the tonic to finally sort out Mrs Gann's unfortunate anal problem.

Chapter Four

THE TORTURE GARDEN

'Beauty is the mistress, the gardener her slave.'
(Michael P. Garofalo)

Barry was ripped violently from sleep again by his night
terrors. Stumbling into the bathroom, he turned on the
tap and drenched his face, to wash away the haunting. With
his father's voice still ringing in his ears, his thoughts turned
to the events of the day before. *What the hell had happened to
Timmy? I'm bound to get the blame. How long before the police
find me?*

He looked up at a painting on the wall his father had
given him the day before he had disappeared. A beautiful
Japanese temple perched on a hillside in an ancient pine
forest. It had three floors, each with its own balcony
possessing intricately carved railings. On the roof was a metal
spire that rose high above the tree line, glistening in the afternoon sun.

At the bottom of the picture was an inscription:

を見つけて

Countless hours had been spent trying to decipher what it meant but there seemed to be a gap where the first character should be, making it awkward to translate. The best Barry had arrived at so far was 'Can't find me.'

Barry came into the kitchen for breakfast and found Molly staring out of the window again. 'Morning.'

'Did you know that no birds fly over Auschwitz?' Molly replied. 'They must sense the inexplicable void of horror that exists there.'

Barry was really not in the mood.

'It's a lovely morning though, Mum. What are you up to today?'

'Merrill's coming over. I'm going to play her Cattle Decapitation's new album.'

'She's in for a treat.' Barry winked.

'I'm sick of being the only OAP metal head in Portslade. I want someone to go to gigs with. You never want to come!'

Barry sat down next to his mum and tried to produce his sweetest smile albeit through the medium of a gappy grin.

'Here we go! What do you want?' said Molly.

'The doctor has prescribed me some supportive under-wear and I'm a bit embarrassed about going in to collect them as that girl I dated, Joanna Tarry, works there. It would be really weird, I haven't spoken to her in years.'

'No way mate! They'll think they're for me! If they get wind of that in the hairdressers the whole town will know!'

Barry knew he had to up his game for this to pan out in his favour; no amount of humbugs would swing this deal.

'How about I buy us tickets to go and see Sepultura in London next week and I'll come with you?'

'Really? Really really?!' shrieked Molly, skipping around the kitchen sounding like a parrot that had just won the lottery.

'Just make sure you get the lycra ones with the velcro side-fasteners, just in case I need to get them off quickly. I don't think I've got time for breakfast now, I'm late for work.'

'Okay, dear, but before you go, do you know what a GILF is? Robbie called me it in the hairdressers the other day and everyone laughed.'

Barry turned and shook his head as he opened the front door. 'It's a grandma I'd like to... oh I really must get off now, Mum. I'll see you later.'

Saturday. Typically, Barry only worked half a day and then went up to his allotment. He was not supposed to but he often stayed the night in his shed to give himself a weekend of undisturbed peace. I say 'undisturbed' but the exception to that rule was Brian. Brian owned the plot adjacent to Barry and was a one-man war machine dedicated to ridding humanity of the wicked pestilence known as weeds.

Some Saturday mornings, Barry would go round to trim Doctor Harper's hedges, a job Barry had been doing once a month since he began gardening. Mrs Harper loved having Barry over for two reasons. Firstly because she had something of an obsession for keeping her hedges immaculately pruned, taking personal offence when nature intervened and caused her hedges to grow. Secondly because she loved talking – I mean really loved talking. It was as if she had a compulsive fear of gaps in a conversation, leading her to develop a manic rhetorical vocal loop. This was one of the instigating factors that had driven Doctor Harper into the garden many years earlier, where he had an office built to see clients privately at the weekends. Mrs Harper found this particularly frustrating due to her confinement indoors as a result of being electronically tagged by East Sussex police. Having frittered away their savings on television shopping channels in the space of six months, she had been subsequently arrested for stealing a packet of crumpets from the corner shop.

One Saturday, Mrs Harper was particularly concerned about the wellbeing of both her pond and hedges.

'There are two main jobs to do today, Barry. The first is we have a leaking pond; I'd like you to empty it and put down a new liner. We have left out our old diesel pump by my husband's cabin which you can use for the draining of the water. Hubby swears it works fine but I'm wary about how safe it is. Please make sure you switch it off as soon as the pond runs dry as it has a tendency to overheat.'

'Okay, Mrs—'

'Now, the hedge, Barry. The left end looks like it's gone a funny colour and I've read that Box blight is sweeping across the south coast. If this is what it is, it would be a disaster. It's a fungus, you know. It causes all the leaves to fall off and never grow back. My neighbour, Mr Pelling, has a bald hedge! It's a catastrophe. He's beside himself.'

'Yes,' replied Barry, 'but, it may just be—'

'Make sure you cut off all the yellowing leaves – they might be infected.'

'Yes, however it might just—'

'Pick up all the old leaves too as the spores can stay alive for years.'

'Yes, Mrs Harper, but—'

'I don't know what I'll do with myself if it is blight, Barry. I won't be able to look my neighbours in the eye!'

Barry tried again. 'It's probably just—'

'The pump is very close to the back window of my husband's cabin so please try not to make too much noise. He has a client over today and they're doing some very important work.'

'Okay, Mrs—'

'I'll be watching from the conservatory. Give me an update as soon as you can.'

Barry opened the back door to give the non-verbal cue that he was leaving this conversational carnage. He got his body out the door then quickly shouted back, 'Your hedge may just have wind damage.'

As Barry disappeared into the back garden, he could hear Mrs Harper redirecting her verbal onslaught towards the long-suffering family dog.

Barry got out his tools and set to work on the sorry-looking hedge. As he was chopping away, his shears seemed to be making a train like noise. It took him back to a day trip he had taken with his sister, Mindy, up to London. They were having an outing to Madam Tussauds wax museum that Molly had organised. It was her hope that the trip might bring the siblings closer together.

About midway through their journey, Mindy had spotted a large bag leaning over the side of the luggage rack adjacent to where they were sitting. The bumpy train ride was causing the bag to creep off the edge of the rack where below an unsuspecting man was eating a sandwich. Mindy kept nudging and repeating to Barry, 'It's about to fall, it's about a fall, it's going to be hilarious!' Barry looked over, got up and walked to the man to warn him of the imminent danger.

The man took the bag off the rack and put it on the ground next to him. This was incomprehensible to Mindy: to her, it justified all the criticism she had ever directed towards her brother. *Barry the destroyer of fun. The boy incapable of making friends.*

Although this was a painful memory for Barry, the most frustrating part about it was that he was never given the chance to explain his actions. When he had looked over at the guy, he noticed a bowling ball emblem on his t-shirt. His companions on the train all had the same t-shirts, leading Barry to the assumption that they were a bowling team on their way to a competition. Barry further deduced that there was a strong chance that the man's bag contained a bowling ball. Should this have landed on his head it could well have killed him. But Mindy's endorphin-seeking mind would probably not have been changed by such trivial details anyway.

Barry returned to his shearing. Standing back to admire his work, Barry let out a short yelp when he saw Terry the Hedge's big eyes looking up at him.

'Afternoon, guvnor! 'Ow's it going?'

'Christ, you almost gave me a heart attack! Couldn't you give me a warning or something? Anyway, I want to apologise for the way I spoke to you last time; it was just all a bit weird.'

'No need to apologise, squire. What's been happening?'

'Things have been much weirder. I've been having nightmares, warning me about samurai ghosts. Wherever I go, people start acting crazy and I've been getting these rages. It's all too much.'

'Your anger is a symptom. What you're seeking is your true calling in the world – your own inner ninja – but you can only discover that when you've found out what's happened to your father, isn't that right?'

'I suppose... How do you know that?

'Whether you know it or not, you are the chosen one to complete the ninja prophecy.'

'What's that?' Barry put down his shears.

'You have been following it for years without even knowing it. It's all around you, yet you don't recognise it... It gives you hope... It's what carries you through the day. It is a path that has been laid down for you, and you alone, for hundreds of years!'

Barry took in a deep breath to help him process what he was hearing. 'My dad used to sing me this lullaby every night, "forget everything you think you know, catch the sun and make it snow." Do you know what it means?'

'Only you can answer that.'

'How? Is my dad still alive?'

'That is your quest. I know this ain't easy to understand. When the time is right, I'll give you a riddle. Should you solve it, you'll be on your way to fulfilling the prophecy. Should you fail, you will be destined to live ten thousand more lifetimes as a gardener.'

'Fuck me. I'm not sure I like those odds! I don't want any part of it!'

'Too late for that, me old mukka. The cosmic wheels have already been set in motion. One last thing... I left you something.'

'What?'

'A sat nav.'

'What do I need one of them for?'

'It's a sat nav with an important difference. It don't take you to where you want to go, it takes you where you need to go to.' With that, Terry disappeared into a puff of green smoke, leaving Barry to get his head round this new information.

Mrs Harper leant out of her kitchen window and shouted, 'Is that a fungus spore I can see exploding?'

Sitting down with a cup of tea from his flask, Barry thought, *Why couldn't I channel a native American elder? Or an Inuit priest? What do I get? A bloody barrow boy!*

Barry picked up his shears, hoping he could now get on

with some work. Gardening was the only thing that seemed remotely normal.

No sooner had he started than he sensed another presence. He turned round and saw Doctor Harper standing inappropriately close, looking like his feathers had been rustled. The doctor grabbed Barry by the arm and stared intensely into his eyes. He spoke as if about to impart information of the gravest importance.

'Barry, dear boy, I've got myself in a bit of a quandary and a rather delicate situation has arisen. I run an informal sex clinic for some of my clients on the weekends. Do you remember Joanna Tarry? although she now likes to be known as Madam Zanzibar. She's come to me today, Barry, desperate for help. I'm trying to realign her sexual needs into healthier areas. Before I can do this, we first need to explore why she is acting out the way she does. To be brutally honest, she needs a playmate.'

'How could I forget Jo, she was my girlfriend for a while. It was a long time ago now, but it's probably not appropriate for me to take part. What kind of playmate are you talking about?'

'Oh, it's nothing to worry about, Barry. Just a few silly games that will highlight to me some of the power struggles she needs to let go of. If you feel uncomfortable at any point, just say the word "enough" and it will all stop.'

'I'm not sure how comfortable I feel about this, doctor. As I say, I haven't seen her for a long time, and anyway, I'm draining the pond and need to switch off the pump soon.'

Doctor Harper threw his arm around Barry and directed him towards his cabin.

'It won't take long, Barry, and it may even help you with some of your anger issues, you never know. Just one thing... I will need you to act out a character in order for Madame Zanzibar to accept you as her playmate. She is what is known as a dominatrix so I will have to dress you up a bit too. Some of the terms may be confusing but I'll explain things as we go.'

'Oh, I don't want to get dressed up.'

'Don't worry. It's only a couple of accessories. To start with, I need you to play the role of human furniture.'

'What?'

'Something you can put your feet on like a footstool.'

'You want me to pretend to be a footstool?'

'Precisely, Barry, my boy! But first I need you to slip on this mono-glove.'

'What the—'

Doctor Harper bent him forwards and strapped both his arms behind him into the leather arm-binder. He then guided Barry face-first to the floor with his backside sticking up in the air. 'Just one last thing. I need you to just pop this on too.'

Barry's head was then strapped into a leather head harness which had a built-in ball gag causing him to retch. In an attempt to struggle free, Barry sat up but the doctor pushed him straight back down to the floor.

'Come now, Barry, were nearly there.' With this, he hit a big gong in the corner of the room.

A door opened at the rear of the cabin and Barry could hear a clack clack clack as someone stomped across the wooden floor towards him. Barry endeavoured to look up but could only see a pair of thigh-high PVC boots in front of him. The boots walked around him: clack, clack, clack, like a hunter sniffing out its pray. Barry went to speak but the ball gag made him choke every time he opened his mouth.

Then a steely voice commanded. 'I am Zanzibar! I am your ruler and your goddess! I will show you little mercy! And if you beg me, I will show you even less! Oh is that you, Barry? How long has it been? I didn't know this was your bag.

Are we gonna have some fun!' She then bashed Barry round
the head with a big padded wet sock.

Barry kept turning his head to protect himself but was
overwhelmed by a foul stench. He looked towards the doctor
and mumbled as best he could, 'Whus huppenin?'

'It's what's known in the trade as a Hot Carl.'

'Whut's hot curl?'

'In layman's terms, it's a sock full of fresh excrement,
Barry.'

'Whut!' Barry tried to jerk free but Madame Zanzibar
jacked his head back and painted a hot wet liquid on to his
upper lip.

'Ah, I see you have gone for the Dirty Sanchez. An interesting choice.'

The doctor bent down to whisper in Barry's ear. 'That's a
moustache made of excrement. How are you finding it all so
far? Enjoying yourself?'

Barry glared at the doctor from his shit-battered face, his
lip frantically quivering as he did his best to scream, 'Get me
ourra here!' He could hear the pump outside the window
making a warning noise to signal that it had finished draining
the pond.

'Pomp, pomp,' Barry groaned.

'Come along now, Barry. There will be plenty of time for
rumpy pumpy later. There's still a few more hoops to go
through first. Come on, don't be shy, man.' Zanzibar bent
down and zipped open a big leather bag. 'So, my darling
Doctor Death. What is next on the menu of bastard
delights?'

Doctor Harper leaned in towards Barry. 'Don't worry
about the name, it's just a little private joke we have.'

The doctor then pulled down a harness fixed to the ceiling. He hooked it to the top of the mono-glove and Barry was
thrust mid-air, legs akimbo.

'How do you like my love sling, Barry? What say you, Zanzibar?'

'I think the time has come for the metal intruder, Doctor, don't you?'

Barry was thrashing around in the sling at the same time as trying to see out the window. He could hear the pump overheating as it spluttered and made a sharp wining sound.

'Looks like we have got ourselves a wriggler, Doctor.'

'Come along now, Barry, be brave. There's a good lad,' said the doctor. 'This could help with your bowels.'

Madame Zanzibar was just about to bury the intruder deep into Barry when a loud bang went off just outside the window. She walked over to see what the problem was, placing the intruder on the windowsill as she peered out at the pump. 'Maybe we should turn that thing off?'

'Nonsense. That machine has been running for forty years without incident. Sod this. It's about time I got in on the action!'

Barry, now apoplectic, screeched a muffled complaint through the gag.

'Enuf! enuf! enuf!'

'What's that, Barry? Are you saying rough? You want it more rough? Okay, Zanzibar. It's time we unleashed the demon!'

'You don't mean...'

'Oh yes I do! It's time for the Cleveland steamer, and I'm the very man for the job.'

Madam Zanzibar unhooked the harness, sending Barry crashing to the floor. Before he knew it, the doctor was standing over him with his trousers round his ankles.

'Here it comes!' grunted the doctor who began shaking uncontrollably, his body folding in on itself, contorting, as white foam dripped from his mouth. Barry looked up horrified to see he was clenching a long serrated knife, poised ready to plunge it into him. His eyes had turned into revolving fireballs spitting ash as he growled slowly in Japanese. 'Eigo no otoko wa shinanakereba naranai.' Barry knew exactly what this meant. 'The English man must die!'

Just as the doctor was about to strike, the pump exploded with a thunderous roar. The impact blew the window in, sending the intruder flying across the room and straight into the back of the doctor's head. He hit the ground with a dull thud and an eerie stillness filled the room.

Madam Zanzibar unzipped Barry and took off his gag. 'Do you think he's dead?'

'He has a twelve-inch steel vibrator buried into the back of his head so if I were to hazard a wild guess—'

'Oh no, my dear doctor, I can't lose you!' She turned to Barry. 'Where shall we hide the body?'

'That must have been the shortest bereavement in history. Why do we need to hide him? This was a clear case of death by vibrator.'

Zanzibar grabbed Barry desperately by the arm.

'You don't understand, I'm already on the run from the police... due to another accident I had...'

'Yeah, actually it's the same for me. Let's stick him under the new pond liner. The bump won't notice once I get the plants back in.'

Barry set about his work while Madam Zanzibar cleaned up all traces of the afternoon's activities. Dragging the lifeless body into the pond, Barry was careful to avoid Mrs Harper's line of sight. He wondered how long it would take before she called the police, two or three days?

An hour later, Barry came back into the cabin. 'It's time to leave. I'll sneak out the back gate first then you follow ten minutes later. Never mention a word of this to anyone. You will never see me again.'

'Before you go, Barry, would you like to try some CBT?'

'Cognitive behavioural therapy?' replied Barry.

'No, I mean cock-and-ball torture.'

'No, thank you, Joanna. I think it's time I left the country. Also I think there's probably something quite drastically wrong with you.'

Barry went home, knowing he couldn't stay there. It was only a matter of time before the police would come looking for him. He decided to go and hide out in his allotment shed until he could get his head straight. Molly was at Bingo so he packed some bags and left a short note:

Dear Mum,

I've done some things I'm not proud of and now I have to go into hiding for a while.

I'm really sorry .

I love you.

Barry

P.S. Please use up the rest of my fish fingers.

P.P.S I'm going to try and find Dad and Mindy.

Chapter Five

THE PORTSLADE MASSACRE

By his own estimation, Robbie Jarvis was the most talented lover in the known universe. He was also pretty well known in the world of hairdressing. Articles had been written on his revolutionary scissor-over-comb technique which really challenged the accepted paradigms within the arena of elderly hair care. Robbie was the only hairdresser in the southeast to offer a five-day crumple-free guarantee on his shampoo and sets. (In many cases the hairstyle would actually outlive the customer.) Robbie claimed the secret of this follicle rigidity was all in the roller technique and not in the half tin of hairspray he used.

Robbie's vision of sexual utopia could be neatly symbolised by a jar of pickled gherkins. The longer the jar sat on your shelf, the sweeter tasting the gherkins, although it was a lot harder to get the lid off – a potentially controversial view yet one he was happy to share with the old ladies at the Astral Waves hair salon.

'Ooh you are naughty,' said Molly. 'You remind me of my Yamochi; he was like a wild dog when we were in our twenties. I had to keep him on a leash. Can you do my hair like Jennifer Lopez has hers?'

Robbie held his scissors up in the air. 'I might look like a wizard, darling, but these ain't no magic wand!' The whole salon erupted with laughter.

'You cheeky bugger,' replied Molly.

Robbie grabbed a handful of curlers and set to work.

'I think everyone should experiment sexually a bit,' said Molly. 'My husband spent years trying to get me to lez up with Merril when she was living above the funeral directors. I eventually gave it a go. It was all right, I suppose. The smell of formaldehyde put me off a bit, mind.'

Two miles north of Portslade High Street, Barry was hiding away in his allotment shed contemplating his situation. *What the hell is after me? Shall I hand myself in? How long do I have before the police find me? What would Dad do?*

Barry knew he had to lay low but didn't want to be far from Molly; he was worried about how she would cope on her own. He remembered that in the garden behind Robbie's salon was an old war bunker that he used to play in when he was a child. If he could get into that and hide, it might buy him a bit of time. Barry tried to sneak out of his shed and make it to the water tap when he was cornered by Brian.

'Ah, Barry. Have you read the allotment newsletter this month? The management committee are suggesting that we use landscape fabric to mulch our plots as a preventative weed measure. That's the most ridiculous suggestion I've ever heard as it's mainly dandelions we have here. I phoned the allotment officer, Mr Baldwin, to express my alarm and told him in no uncertain terms that this was an exercise in pure folly.' Brian edged his way closer to Barry to deliver the vital ingredient in his riposte.

'Did you know a dandelion cracked open my patio? I put this to Mr Baldwin and do you know what he said?' Barry opened his mouth to reply but Brian steamed on. 'He said he was aware the plant had a strong "growth force" and with that I just burst out laughing, Barry. Of course I had to explain to him that he was confusing "growth force" with "root pressure" which is an entirely different volitional kettle of fish.'

Barry was not listening. He was staring off into the distance, daydreaming. *Why did Doctor Harper chant in Japanese? He looked possessed. This must be what my dad was warning me about in my dream.* Brian continued rabbiting away to himself in the background until Barry eventually brought his mind back momentarily to ponder, *I wonder if Brian is the most boring man in the universe?*

Barry eventually escaped the allotment policy inquest and prepared himself for the journey back to town.

Darkness had set in by the time he mustered up enough confidence to leave the safety of his shed. It was a quiet Sunday night; the only sounds were the occasional buses going up and down the High Street.

Donning his ninja mask and black kimono, Barry slinked his way via parks and back gardens to avoid detection.

On arriving at the rear of the salon, he cautiously climbed over the back gate and made his way through the shrub borders and down the steps to the sunken bunker door. A new steel-framed door had been erected since he was there. His heart sank. There was no way he'd gain entry. The clang of steel boomeranged around the garden as Barry kicked at it hopelessly. He flumped to the ground and lay back on the grass, looking up at the stars. Never had he felt more lost and alone.

That's it, he thought. *I'm going to hand myself in, I'm going to go upstairs, tell Mum what's happened, then call the police.*

As he walked back to the gate, he heard a tapping noise. He walked all around the garden but could see nothing through the blur of night.

The tapping grew louder and Barry realised it was coming from the bunker door. He pressed his ear against the door.

'Is anyone in there?'

'Yes,' came a muffled response.

'Speak up. I can't hear you.'

'What are you doing in the garden?'

'I should be asking what you are doing in there?'

'This is where I live,' replied the indignant voice.

'How long have you been in there?'

'I don't know... years and years.'

'Are you a prisoner?'

'No, not at all. Robbie invited me down here to—'

An ice-cold shiver swept over Barry.

'Mindy?'

'Barry?'

'Mindy, what the hell are you doing in there?' Tears started falling from his eyes.

'I've been looking after a gang of slow lorises.'

'What the hell are they?' Barry yanked at the door joints as forcefully as he could but it failed to budge.

'They're cute little furry creatures with funny sausage fingers.'

'Just wait till I get hold of Robbie. Have you been looked after? How are you?'

'How am I? I don't know. It's been so long since I thought about it really. Robbie bestowed upon me the honorary title of Loris Protector and I've sworn a lifetime oath to serve—'

'Mindy, you've been fucking kidnapped.'

'A Loris Protector is a very important job, you know! Robbie has kindly given me a DVD player that has a documentary on slow lorises, I've seen it eight thousand three hundred and twenty-two times. Sometimes I pretend to be a loris and my friend Big Mandy has kindly built me a wooden platform so I can perch near them. Not inside their cage though as they are pretty deadly!'

Barry felt his stomach tightening as he brushed the tears from his eyes.

'Mindy, what the hell is going on?'

'What do you mean? Did you know that loris is Dutch for clown?'

She's lost her tiny mind, thought Barry. *I've got to get her out of there.* Barry looked towards the back of the salon.

'Okay, Mindy. I'm going to try to find the key to get you out of there.'

'Okay, Barry. Please be careful of Big Mandy if you see him. He isn't friendly with everyone.'

Barry gradually made his way over to the back door of the salon and looked up to where he could see a window open about six metres up from the back door of the building. One of the best-kept secrets of a ninja was how they could scale the walls of a castle seemingly unaided. This secret was a set of metal claws that you could strap to the bottom of your feet. As luck would have it, Barry's friend Tom was a dab hand at metal work and had made some for him by smelting down a pair of his rusty old shears. Barry strapped them on and climbed up the rear wall of the salon. He grabbed hold of the window ledge and slowly put his hand into the window to open it fully.

Before he had a chance to climb in, a light went on and a large man with crimson cheeks, wild protruding eyes and a colossal beard appeared at the window. This was no ordinary beard; it was as if a particularly invasive rhododendron had colonised his face.

Losing his grip and exchanging the ledge for two handfuls of beard, Barry let out a short scream. 'Ahh! Fuck me!'

'Let go, you little bastard,' the man growled, trying to hold onto the upper part of his beard to stop having his chin pulled off. Barry could see another window ledge to his right, which he decided was the only place he could possibly reach. He swung on the beard to gain enough momentum to successfully make the leap. Having Barry's fat arse swinging from his beard was pulling the man further and further out of the window.

'What the hell are you trying to do?' howled the man, tears streaming from his eyes.

Just as Barry was about to take his lunge, he heard the rasping sound of beard tearing from chin, after which he found himself freefalling through the Portslade night clutching two handfuls of wiry beard.

Barry hit the lawn with a sharp thud and then... nothing.

Barry awoke handcuffed to a wall in the bunker next to Mindy. She was staring at him adoringly with an emoji smile that took up her entire face. Apart from having hair that touched the floor and a t-shirt the colour of Gollum's under-pants, she looked as though she hadn't aged a single day. Barry couldn't take his eyes off her. Across the room was a cage with ten motionless slow lorises intently observing their new visitor. The large man from the evening before stood directly in front of Barry, sporting flared nostrils, a satanic glare, and half a beard.

'That's my friend Mandy I was telling you about, Barry,'

whispered Mindy. 'He doesn't speak much. I think you might have upset him, try not to look at him.' Mandy turned his back and walked out of the bunker, slamming the door behind him.

'Mindy, that guy is not your friend and we have to get the fuck out of he—' Barry choked on his words. 'Here. He's going to kill me.'

'But this is where I live, Barry. Did you know they have found nine different species of slow lorises?'

Barry's blood quickened and whirled through his veins. He grabbed Mindy and exploded,

'Come back to me, come back to me!'

'But, Barry, I'm alrigh—'

'No you're not, you've lost your fucking marbles!' Barry shook his sister wildly until she crumpled like a rag doll to the floor, weeeping inconsolably. Barry knelt down and hugged her tighter than he could remember ever having done so.

'I'm sorry... I'm sorry.'

'Don't be sorry, just come back to me.'

'I've been so lost, so very lost...' Mindy wiped her snotty nose with a corner of the t-shirt she had been living in all those years.

'What have they been doing to you in here?'

'I've spent the last twenty-five years playing games with Mandy and looking after these creatures.'

'What kind of games?'

'Whatever Mandy is in the mood for: Twister, Scrabble, you name it. Robbie joins in sometimes – he likes to play a game called sploshing.'

'What the hell is that?'

'It's some weird thing he's into; he turns up with bags of cream buns, chocolate puddings, custard tarts and raw eggs. The object of their game is to throw these things at me until I'm covered from head to foot. I think he gets off on it.'

'Jesus... and why does he keep these slow lorises?'

'Robbie takes them round to visit the old ladies he's been sleeping with after he's convinced them to include him in their will. Slow lorises secrete a deadly venom from their armpits which they lick before biting their victims. If you didn't know that, you couldn't help but cuddle them... the poor old dears. Robbie says the venom is untraceable; it just looks like a heart attack. He thinks he's invented the perfect murder.'

'What a bastard. Did you know that Dad went missing the same day as you did?'

'I did see him on my way home from work and he told me that he had to go away for a while. He said something really odd, that his ninja family were in need of him and he had to go and help them. Do you know what that means?'

'I haven't a clue, but I'm going to find out. Mindy, I have to tell you I've got myself into a lot of trouble and the police are after me.'

'What have you—'

The conversation was interrupted as Robbie and Mandy entered the bunker.

'So, Mandy, have we caught ourselves a naughty boy?'

'Yes, boss.'

'And what happens to naughty boys and girls, Mandy?'

'I play with them, boss.'

'Exactly! You play with them, and what happens when you play with them?'

'Sometimes I break them, boss.' Robbie's head tilted back to let out a loud self-satisfied laugh.

'You're clumsy aren't you, Mandy.'

'Yes, boss.'

Mandy unfolded a plastic mat on the floor and said to Mindy, 'Mandy is going to play Twister with you first.'

'I don't fancy my chances of getting out of this, Barry,'

said Mindy anxiously. 'I need you to know I would never have left you on purpose and I love you.'

Mandy unlocked Mindy's handcuffs and pushed her down onto the Twister mat.

'Do you want me to go first, Mandy?' asked Mindy.

'No, Mandy's going to go first and last.' And with, that he jumped on top of her and got her into a strangle hold. If any of Barry's ninja training was ever to mean anything, now was the time he most needed to draw upon it. He dislocated his wrist and carefully slid it out of the handcuff, ran over and jumped on Mandy's back whilst poking two fingers in his eyes.

'Argh!' screamed Mandy as he dropped Mindy and threw Barry against the wall. He picked up a baseball bat, a sinister smile lighting up his face.

'Would you like to play a game of rounders with me, Barry?'

'Over my dead body!' screamed a voice in the doorway. Everyone looked up.

Molly was standing in the entrance with ten other ladies from the salon. Each one was sporting curlers, hairnets, and an assortment of Barry's ninja weapons. Molly growled at Robbie,

'So you've been holding my daughter captive all these years, have you?'

'No, not really. It's what she wanted, darling. She was helping me look after my pets.'

Molly had a certain look in her eye. A look that took you back to that fateful day of the Emmerdale plane crash. A look born of twenty-five long years of brooding and unresolved grief. A look that was about to find some unexpected resolution. Revolving her nunchucks, she addressed her posse.

'Ladies, I've been around for a long time. You all know me well. I've come to understand there is one great inescapable truth in this life. That truth, my friends, is justice. Like all great reckonings, it doesn't come very often. But when it does, it is quick, brutal, and very bloody. Prepare yourselves for an OAP armageddon. Charge!'

Molly ran full pelt at Robbie with the rest of the old dears in her wake. It was unremitting and relentless carnage; there were metal chains, samurai swords and hair curlers flying everywhere. Dispensing with her nunchucks, Molly jumped on Robbie's back, deciding instead to head-butt him until further notice. Mandy played trampolines on top of two old dears who were looking a little the worse for wear until Merril took him down with a ninja star between the eyes.

Mandy fell backwards, crashing into the cage of slow lorises, which immediately swarmed over him, ripping little chunks of flesh from his body. He struggled momentarily, before falling silent in a bloody heap on the floor.

Molly hobbled over to her ladies.

'Did you see where Robbie went? One minute I was head-butting him, the next he just vanished... into thin air!' She reached down and helped Mindy up off the Twister mat.

'Be a good girl and give your old mum a hug.' They embraced, sobbing long lost tears into each other's shoulders. Mindy seemed to be slowly emerging from her trance.

'I've missed you so much, Mum... so very very much.'

'I know dear, I know.'

Barry walked around checking everyone was okay, then stopped and put his arm around Merril.

'How did you know we were in here?'

'I live across the road from the bakers and have been getting very suspicious with all the cream buns Robbie was buying. Molly saw him bringing them back here from her kitchen window and we knew he had to be up to no good.'

'That's what you've been staring at all this time, mum!'

Barry started picked up the weapons from the floor. 'We need to cover our tracks and get rid of this body.'

'I know where they keep the spare key for the undertakers,' said Merril. 'I think we could add his body to a coffin that's awaiting burial. What do you think?'

Molly found a hose-pipe and began spraying the blood-stains off the bunker walls.

'I can't think of a better plan. There's a wheelbarrow in the garden – we could use that to get him over there.'

Mindy looked at the remains of the slow loris cage. 'The lorises got their revenge on Mandy but it looks like they have escaped! Be on your look out, everyone. Avoid them at all costs.'

The group crept into the back of the undertaker's, dragging one limb each of Mandy's massive corpse. They found a room that had five wooden coffins in it and judging by the smell must have been the embalming room. It had a spectral yet clinical feel to it, maybe what the waiting room for Nosferatu's dentist would be like. Barry carefully unsealed the lid of the largest coffin and, to Molly's surprise, she saw one of her good friends from the hairdressers.

'That's Ada, bless her. Robbie had just turned his attentions towards her.'

'I think it was an accident,' interjected Mindy. 'Mandy suffocated her while they were playing hopscotch together. It's quite fitting they go in the same coffin, but how the hell are we going to get him in there?'

Barry wandered off and returned with some rope, which he looped over a stack of coffins.

'Let's hoist him in, tie the rope round his waist, and we can lower him down on top of Ada. Molly walked over and inspected Mandy's gnarly tuberous face.

'I wonder where it all went wrong for him? He looks so sweet lying there.'

'Yeah, dead sweet,' replied Barry.

Suddenly, Mandy sat up and, through the mass of ripped-up beard, screamed, 'Mandy lives!' His wild protruding eyes surveyed his environment as his demolition truck hands ripped the rope from his torso. He was just about to get up when Barry hit him slap bang in the face with a coffin lid.

'Quick! Follow me.' Barry led everyone out the front door and they ran down the middle of the high street.

Mandy was behind them in hot pursuit, stark bollock naked with a ninja star sticking out of his forehead. He was letting out loud groans as his body convulsed, careering down the road like a truck with withered brake cables. His eyes had changed, they were disused coal mines, dark and vacant. He began a Japanese death chant. 'Eigo no ninja e no shi'

'Whats he saying?' asked Molly gasping for breath.

'Death to the English ninja, I think' replied Barry.

'Who's he referring to?'

'Me, for fuck's sake!' Barry shook his head and pointed to his puffing posse to cross the road. As they reached the end of Portslade High Street they turned the corner to find a group of police officers helping the pest control department round up a gang of slow lorises that had taken residence in some trees outside the post office.

'We're being chased by a naked lunatic!' screamed Molly.

Before the police had a chance to react, Mandy had jumped headfirst into their midst. All hell broke loose; truncheons, handcuffs and tit-shaped hats flew in all directions. The mayhem was the perfect opportunity for Barry to smuggle everyone into the back of a pest control van. They quickly disappeared into the darkness.

'Take us to Ada's house,' Molly ordered. 'She never locked her door, no one will find us there.'

. . .

As soon as they arrived at Ada's, Barry jumped out of the van and embraced Molly and Mindy.

'I love you both with all my heart, but I have to carry on. I'm on a journey and I need to see where it takes me. Please don't worry. I'll be back soon, hopefully with some answers about Dad.'

'You're a good boy Barry,' said Molly with tears in her eyes.' By the way I didn't manage to buy you anymore of your nappies, I'm afraid.'

'They are not nappies mum and you haven't told anyone have you?'

'I mentioned it to a few of the girls at the hairdressers but they aren't likely to tell anyone.' Said Molly sheepishly.

'It's a good job I'm leaving isn't it!' Mindy grabbed Barry and hugged him as tightly as she could. 'I'm sorry I was so cruel to you. Can you ever forgive me?'

'None of that matters now. All I care about is having you back. Are you two going to be okay?'

'Don't you worry about us,' replied Molly, 'We've got twenty five years of catching up to do, haven't we, Mindy, and there's this great band I've been getting into called Knife Thru Head. I can't wait to play them to you.'

Barry got back in the van and plugged in the sat nav Terry had given him. A jingle started playing that sounded like a child's xylophone, that was soon interrupted by an ethereal voice.

'Hello and welcome to Cosmic Sat Navs Incorporated, a transcendental knowledge highway support guide brought to you by the Prophecy Allocation Department. We are proud to say we've been taking sentient life forms to where they *need* to go since the dawn of creation.'

Barry drove off into the night. He was being directed

down seemingly endless winding country lanes. He appeared to be headed northbound towards London, but he could have been anywhere. The monotony was stupefying. By the time the journey ended, Barry could barely keep his eyes open. He clambered into the back of the van and fell into a deep sleep.

Chapter Six

MOLLY'S KNOCKERS

Barry awoke early the next morning, his face pressed hard up against the frosty metal shell of the van. He had produced a small stream of dribble that was making its way down the oily steel into layers of animal hair and crisp wrappers below. He peered out of the rear window and saw he was parked outside a tall grey building. One of those 1950s office blocks that looked like a giant lump of concrete no one had bothered to paint. There was a large bronze sculpture of a muscular man on the forecourt. The immaculately designed figure had one hand on his heart and the other pointing upward to the heavens. Barry bought himself a coffee from a nearby kiosk and sat down to look at the sculpture. He had a conflicted relationship with art; it nearly always intrigued him though he felt it was only intended for those who had been educated to understand and profit from it. The man's expression seemed to convey a deep torment, just how Barry felt a lot of the time.

He looked up at the sign above the building entrance, which read "The South London Centre for Experimental Psychotherapy". *Why would Terry bring me here?* thought Barry.

This is where Doctor Harper referred me to, wasn't it? Is this a trap? If it is, I'll cut down every hedge on the south coast! That'll shut him up!

Barry slid softly through the revolving front doors of the entrance in deep ninja stealth mode, reducing his breathing to one inhalation a minute to register no atmospheric trace. If it weren't for the CCTV cameras this may have been quite an effective strategy. *There's no way I'm taking the lift. You leave yourself far too vulnerable.* Barry started the long walk up the spiral staircase to the psychotherapy offices at the top of the building.

The acoustics of this vast concrete and steel stairwell were such that each clang of Barry's gardening boots seemed to merge with the next, reverberating and growing ever louder as he progressed upwards. This noise became entwined with his own rising anxiety levels the higher he climbed. *What if the police are waiting for me up there? How will I escape?*

Barry arrived at the top floor and approached an office door that had the name Doctor Thomas Gilpgünter inscribed on the front of it. He knocked as quietly as he could, hoping he wouldn't be heard. A tall man with a grey moustache and monocle appeared at the door. Despite his anxiety, Barry retained his ninja mindset, sharp and alert, poised for action.

'Can I help you?' he asked abruptly.

'I'm Barry Harris. My GP, Doctor Harper, referred me to you.'

'Do you have an appointment?'

'No.'

'You can't just show up, Mr Harris. I'm really very busy. I'm supposed to be writing up my case notes this morning.'

'I wasn't quite sure I was coming here... It's difficult to explain... I've come a long way.'

The doctor paused a moment, removed his monocle, then

ushered Barry into the room. 'Come in, come in and take a seat. Help yourself to some water.'

Barry sat down and picked up a jug of water but it slipped through his fingers, crashing down on the table.

'Be careful! Be careful! Please relax, Mr Harris. There is really nothing to worry about.'

'I'm sorry. I've had a rough few days.'

The doctor sat down on a chair opposite Barry. 'Listen, I'll make an exception and see you this once, as you are here. This is an exception though do you understand?

'Yes, of course.'

'OK well, First I will tell you about myself. Please call me by my first name, which is Thomas. May I call you Barry?' Barry nodded and gave a weary smile.

'I have been living in England for forty years but was born in Switzerland. I come from a tradition of psychoanalysis dating back to a famous therapist by the name of Carl Jung. Tell me, Barry, did you see the statue on our forecourt? I had this commissioned especially.'

'Yes. I sat down to look at it. I found it quite compelling.' Barry reclined in his chair, trying to relax.

'What did it make you think of when you looked at it?'

'There's something quite powerful but a bit dark about it.'

Thomas got up to walk over to the window to observe his masterpiece.

'Ah, interesting! It represents our shadow self. There are shadows in all of us which are the nasty or painful aspects we spend our lives hiding from. We project these parts of ourselves onto the outside world and they come back and bite us! The statue has one hand on his heart and the other pointing to the stars. It is our job in therapy to hunt out this shadow, make it conscious so we can release its grip on us.' Thomas sprayed his window with a fine mist of spittle as he excitedly assumed the statue's posture. 'I often stare down at that sculpture and wonder what it would be like to be truly integrated with my shadow.'

'Do you think we'll have time to do that for me today?' asked Barry.

'Ha ha. If only that were possible. It's a life's journey but today you take your first steps. So tell me, why have you come to see me?'

'I seem to get myself into trouble without meaning to. I get this extreme anger that takes hold of me and I feel powerless to control it. I've tried all kinds of things to calm myself down but I feel like I'm surrounded by idiots who are constantly provoking me. I try to be a good Buddhist, as compassionate as I can be, but it always seems to get out of hand.'

'I see. Can you remember a time when this problem didn't affect you?'

'That must have been before my father left home twenty-five years ago.'

'I see. I would like to start by doing some hypnosis, if that is okay with you? We need to find out what it is you are running from.'

'I'll try it if you think it will work, Doctor.'

'Yes, yes. It can be very effective. Please make yourself comfortable and close your eyes. Take three slow deep breaths. I want you to visualise yourself walking down a hill towards a beautiful sunny meadow. With every step, you become more and more at peace until eventually you lie down in the long grass and all you can hear is my voice. With every breath, you are falling deeper and deeper into relaxation. You are very safe – nothing can harm you. Are you feeling at peace, Barry?'

'Yes, Thomas.'

'I would like you to speak freely without self-regulation to the questions I ask you. No one is judging you. I would to talk to you about your sex life. Can you remember your earliest sexual experience?'

'I had a snog with Joanna Tarry in the back row of the cinema in 1995. We were watching *Die Hard*.'

'Can you remember the first time you had sex?'

'No...I've.... never had sex.'

'Fascinating! The virgin man, a raging torrent of repressed desires and social humiliation. Why have you waited so long? At this rate you <u>will</u> die hard, Barry. Tell me, were you bottle fed?'

'I can't remember.'

'Do you remember preferring one of your mother's breasts over the other?'

'What?' said Barry, his calm beginning to fray at the edges.

Thomas continued. 'Do you still think about your mother's breasts?'

'What! Leave my mum's tits out of it – she's eighty-two!'

'I believe you may have transferred your latent rage of being denied your mother's breasts into a fear of women. What do you think about when you masturbate?'

Barry could feel himself gripping handfuls of leather upholstery. 'Golf; it helps me last longer.'

'Tell me about your dreams, Barry. Do you ever remember what they are about?'

'I have a reoccurring nightmare where I am hanging off a cliff. There are samurai with swords coming at me and sharp rocks in the ocean below. I can hear my father's voice warning me of danger. I'm scared. I don't know what to do.'

'Fascinating! Maybe your hanging from a cliff is a metaphor for the memory of your father. You must let go! Let go!'

'No, I can't. He's still alive. I know he is!' Barry's heartbeat quickened.

'He's never coming back. You must move on. Let go! Let go!'

'No!' Barry's lip was quivering, he gripped the arms of the chair as if to stop himself falling.

'If you stay on the cliff you will never heal, Barry. Let go!'

'I'll never let go and I'll never give up!'

Thomas went quiet. Then, standing up, he grabbed a huge plant pot and lifted it high above Barry's head. Black lumpy sludge was spewing out of his mouth and he spluttered a coarse monotone chant in Japanese. 'Watashi wa yogen o korosu.' Barry's translation skills were improving, he understood the words instantly. 'I kill the prophecy.'

Barry's eyes sprang open as he jumped to his feet and launched into the most awesome roundhouse that caught Thomas square on the chin. It sent him flying backwards crashing through his office window and hurtling toward to the street below. Barry ran to the window just in time to see Thomas impaled onto the pointing finger of his precious sculpture. Looking at his dangling lifeless body, Barry thought to himself, *at least he now knows what it's like to be fully integrated with his shadow.* His next thought was, *time to leave.*

Barry sneaked out into the hallway of the offices, wondering where that move had come from. His father had taught him ninjutsu, yes, but that was so long ago, and the details were foggy. He only hoped the fog was beginning to lift. About time, considering what he was up against.

A painting in the hallway grabbed his attention. Exactly the same painting of a wooden temple as his father had given him! Only there was something different about this copy. Its inscription read:

私を見つけて

It's got the missing symbol. He read aloud, 'Watashi o

mitsukete' – that doesn't mean "can't find me" it means "come find me"!' Barry threw his arms into the air. 'I knew it!'

He ran to the van and drove without blinking all the way back to his allotment. *If ever I needed spiritual guidance, it's now*, thought Barry as he pulled up in front of his plot.

Hunting through his impossibly overcrowded shed, Barry found a pair of rusty old shears and chopped away at the boundary hedge.

'Afternoon, sparrow. You been busy,' piped up Terry. 'I think I owe you an apology this time. I never thought it was going to kick off with that therapist. It looks like everyone you come into contact with is getting possessed by Cygloar, a demonic samurai ghost!'

Barry drew a deep breath.

'It must be what my dad's been warning me about in my nightmares. I can't take it any longer, I need to get away from here. I know my dad's alive. I just need to find a way to locate him.'

Terry's leaves rustled in the breeze.

'That might be more tricky than what you fink, me old china.'

'What? Is that the best you can do? I need divine intervention! You're supposed to be a spiritual guide, so fucking guide me!'

'All right, geezer, don't get a cob on. How about I give you another riddle?'

'Fuck me, another riddle, you haven't give me the first one yet... Is this a riddle to replace the first riddle?'

'No it's as well as the first riddle, but you could have it before if you like? It could be a pre-riddle riddle.'

'Bloody Nora. Can't you just tell me what I need to know?'

'Sorry, not licensed to, mate. That would be way above me

pay grade. Anyway that's not the way transcendental wisdom works. Where would be the adventure in that?'

'I don't need an adventure. I'm desperate. I really need your help!'

'Okay. Look, I'll tell you what I'll do for you. I'm still gonna give you your first riddle, that's yours to keep and trust me, you'll need it. What I can do you for you today is also give you a conundrum.'

Barry looked at the ground. 'I'm knackered.'

'Don't be like that. I'll walk you through the first riddle. Listen carefully as I'll only say this once. There's a well-known teaching within the Buddhist tradition that goes: "Mindfulness is the Path to the Deathless".'

'Yes I know that but how does that help me?'

'For any meditation master there is an escape hatch from this world of suffering, a gateway to a deathless realm.'

'But I've only been meditating regularly for the last few months,' said Barry. 'I'm definitely no master!'

'That's where I can help, see. I is the undisputed king of shortcuts! All you need to do is go on the internet and buy yourself a mindfulness teacher certificate for twenty quid. You don't even need to have meditated once. As soon as you done that, all you need is to solve the following conundrum: "The transcendental gateway lies beneath the carpet of infinity".'

Bugger me, thought Barry, *it's all prophecies, conundrums and riddles with these ethereal beings.*

Chapter Seven

THE PROPHECY ALLOCATION DEPARTMENT

After possibly his most disturbed night's sleep ever, Barry rose early and circumnavigated a small patch of grass in front of his allotment shed. *I can't think straight, I need to meditate, no I can't concentrate, but I must keep my focus, where can this carpet of infinity be? I need to act fast or I'm a goner.*

Crossing the road from the allotments, Barry went over to the shopping centre and entered a giant discount carpet showroom. He found himself aimlessly running up and down the aisles, not knowing what he was looking for.

A teenage sales assistant appeared from behind the offcuts section. 'Can I help you, sir?'

'Do you have anything called a carpet of infinity, by any chance?'

'We have the Raspberry Infinity Twist range if that's what you mean? It's on special offer at £3.99 a square metre and comes with a one-year stain-free guaran—'

Barry was out the shop and back at the allotments by the time the assistant had finished his sentence. Floating around in a daze, Barry was unable to form even the simplest of thoughts. He was beyond exhausted. Collapsing to his knees, he wept into the soil like a little boy.

'Where are you when I need you most, Dad? Where are you?'

Barry heard a shuffling of feet in front of him and he looked up to see Brian staring down.

'Is everything okay, old chap? You look a little down on your luck if you don't mind me saying.'

'Oh, Brian. Things are little rough for me at the moment... I'm looking for somewhere that has a carpet. Can you think of anywhere?'

'You know I was talking about my perennial weeds the other day?'

'Brian I really haven't got time for weeds now.'

'I think that maybe you do... actually. As you know my dandelions have been reeking havoc on my plot, so much so I got a warning letter about them from the council.'

'Brian, I'm begging you please don't talk to me about weeds.'

'Now hear me out, Barry... Last year, I made a compost bin out of some old wood pallets, filled it with the weeds, mixed in some herbal preparations and used an old carpet to cover it with—'

'Brian I've got to go...'

'Wait! Wait! You haven't heard the really interesting part. I checked to see how the compost was doing about two weeks ago, and realised it had spontaneously turned into a time travel portal.'

Barry opened his mouth but nothing came out.

'Interesting, hey? I naturally figured it must be some kind of intergalactic gateway to an alternative time zone. So I thought I'd try it out – me and the wife have been flying all around the universe. It's exhilarating. We've been into the past... into the future. Last week, we saw the Battle of Hastings. It was a cracking day out.'

Barry opened his mouth again – nothing.

'Come and have a look, old boy.'

Looking like he'd just done a few rounds with Mike Tyson, Barry wobbled over to the compost heap.

'Give me a hand.' Brian pulled back the old rotting carpet from the top of the heap. 'Is this what you were looking for?'

Barry leant over and stared into a deep cavernous expanse in the centre of the heap. It was like looking through a space telescope. Stars were shooting past and there was a large network of transparent tubes going off in all directions. He turned to Brian. 'It's a... er... er.'

'It's amazing is what it is, Barry!'

'Yes... but why is it here?'

'Now that's a very good question. I have a feeling you will need to go in there to find that out. One thing you do need to know though is you don't get to choose where you go.'

'How will I know...' Barry paused as he knelt in front of the hole. 'Where I'm going?'

Brian shrugged and smiled.

'What's all this jelly-like stuff coming out of the bottom of the hole?'

'You need to cover yourself in that before you jump into the tube; it helps you move quicker. There's some kind of suction force that pulls you through the tube.'

'This is what I've been waiting for.' Barry did as he was told then climbed headfirst into the waxy-coated tubing. 'It's like climbing into someone's intestines.'

'You'll soon get used to it, Barry. Get ready... You're about to–'

Barry flew off up the tube, zero to a hundred miles-per-hour in seconds, getting faster and faster, to the point where his cheeks were bulging and tongue flapping wildly out of his mouth. The stars around him blurred and he was having trouble breathing. *Must be reaching the speed of light,* he thought.

The tube criss-crossed with other tubes, a spaghetti junction. He could see other people being pulled in a myriad of directions. Just as he felt he was going to faint, he began slowing down.

With one final slurp, Barry was pumped through the ceiling of a vast open-plan office. Landing with a thud on a grubby old mattress, he found himself looking up at a garish neon sign:

Welcome To The Prophecy Allocation Department.

Taking in his new surroundings, he saw he was in a vast warehouse containing hundreds of rows of seats at one end and five small desks at the other. The place was lit by large strip lights, some of which flickered intermittently, causing a strobe light effect. There was a faint smell of burning flesh from an electric bug zapper on the wall. It was doing a good job of frying any unsuspecting creature that flew within 50cm of it.

A petite but rotund man wearing braces and a pork pie hat helped Barry onto his feet.

'Come along, sir, up you get. We don't like time-wasters here. Take a number and have a seat until you are called.'

Barry looked up at the wall and saw what looked like a clock, except it had two hour hands speeding in different directions that stopped after one rotation and then would go back on themselves making a 'ting!' as they did so. The man sitting next to Barry, who was dressed as Elvis Presley, raised his right eyebrow and introduced himself.

'Hello, I'm Mr Law. I'm here to make a pitch for a new prophecy called "Return to Sender".'

'Hi, I'm Barry. What's that about?'

'I believe that Elvis was a musical genius and it is a catastrophe that we were robbed of his later musical years. I'm proposing to go back in time to save him so he can return and make more beautiful music for us.'

'Save him from who?'

'From himself of course. I have devised some specialised dietary plans for him and I'm even prepared to stay on with him and act as his personal trainer. To be honest with you things haven't been going so great for me lately... the change would do me good. '

'You don't say. Why do you think he's going to be open to you making these changes for him?'

'He's not making a lot of music now, is he?'

Barry tilted his head slightly, frowned, and zoomed in closer to Mr Law.

'So, let me get this straight: you are going to go back in time to save Elvis Presley, from himself, dressed as Elvis Presley? I'm not sure they are going to buy that.'

'Yes, I know it may seem a little odd. It's what's known as a paradoxical intervention.'

'So where does the prophecy come in?' asked Barry.

'If my application is approved, the department have a way of inserting into history (in diaries, letters, old manuscripts, that sort of thing) evidence of the new prophecy. That way, the new prophecy becomes an old prophecy, if you know what I mean. Then I can go on – or back – and fulfill the prophecy, see?'

'No, I don't think I do,' Said Barry, scrunching up his face. 'Try not to go back too early in his career though, you're likely to give him a bloody heart attack.'

A voice blared from the tannoy.

'Number fifty-two to the front desk please.'

Barry approached the front desk to see a tall intense-looking woman staring down at her paperwork. She had the air of a headmistress about her and looked like a cross between Mrs Marple and Morticia from The Addams Family. There was a bronze plaque on the front of the desk which read: "Ms Hannah McCann – Time Vortex Translocation Coordinator".

'That job title's a bit of a mouthful.' Barry grinned as he sat down.

Ms McCann peered up from behind her half-rimmed spectacles.

'It's not just the material world that gets hit by funding cuts, you know. I'm doing three people's jobs here; I'm working my arse to the bone! Fill in this prophecy request application and please make sure you record the correct time of transcendence. People always get that wrong – it's the bane of my life.'

Barry scribbled away frantically while Ms McCann sat back and read his case file, muttering under her breath, 'Ah!... huh...tut tut!...oh, I see... you're the one who put a cat in a blender! Nasty bit of business that. You seem very good at leaving a trail of chaos behind you, Mr Harris.'

'I can explain... It's not my fault, you see. A ninja demon called Cygloar possessed my gardening clients and tried to kill me.'

'Ha, that's a tall story.'

'How can it be any taller than all this?' Said Barry throwing his arms up in the air. Ms McCann got up and leaned forward over her desk, parking herself about an inch away from Barry's face.

'*All this*, I'll have you know, is *perfectly normal*. Was it Terry the Hedge who put you onto the compost gateway?'

'He gave me a conundrum and I had to try and work it out for myself.'

'He's got a lot to answer for, that one. Did you know he used to work for us in accounting? Useless he was and he never stopped talking! He'd drive me to distraction. That's why I gave him a three-minute conversation limit, he'd drive you insane otherwise! Was it Brian that gave you gateway access?'

'Yes I couldn't have done it without him.'

'Ha ha! I bet you thought he was boring, didn't you? The problem is that the compost gateway is meant to be an emergency time travel portal reserved for wizards and space commandos. That said, we do let Brian use it – you've got to give a little bit back. Its main function is to prevent intergalactic conflict. For someone...well...such as yourself, it's the spiritual equivalent of travelling through a cosmic ring piece. You come out the other end with a condition called karma inversion.'

'What the hell is that?' Barry nibbled the quick of his fingernails.

'It's when all the good deeds you have ever done in your life are erased from history and all you are left with is the cat-in-the-blender type stuff.'

'That's a good start then.' quipped Barry whilst trying to covertly adjust the velcro straps on his underwear. 'So, Mr Harris...this brings us to the details of your mission. You'll be tasked with carrying out prophecy number 231/129.4, commonly known as "The Ninja Prophecy". You'll going back to October 1st 1603 to Rim province in Japan, where Obi Nobmearda, an evil warlord, is leading forty thousand samurai warriors into the province to finish off the ninjas. Only four hundred ninjas remain, and their leader Yamochi—'

'Dad's alive! I knew it! I knew it!'

'Yes, we hope so but he's been captured by the samurai.

It's your mission to get into their heavily-defended hilltop temple and rescue your father so the ninja tradition can live on. It's an impossible mission and you're probably the least capable candidate for the job, but you are all we have, so good luck.'

'Cool, this is like a back to the future ninja black ops! I won't let you down. I'm gonna make those samurai suckers pay for what they have done to my family.'

'By the way, did you know that Robbie Jarvis was a wizard?' Ms McCann removed her spectacles and sat back onto her chair.

'You mean he looks like one?'

'No. He's an actual wizard and not only that, he's also a mercenary who was hired by the warlord Obi Nobmearda to wipe out your family and kill you so you couldn't fulfil the prophecy.'

'What? He's been doing my hair since I was five!... He's an *actual* mercenary time-travelling dark wizard?'

'Yes, with a grey-love addiction, you couldn't make it up, could you? You were lucky, he's normally deadly but he got a bit distracted with his old ladies.'

'So it was his porking that saved my bacon!' Barry looked very pleased with himself.

Ms McCann let slip a rare smile to reveal the most glorious set of mustard-coloured teeth. 'You really are quite a basic individual, aren't you?'

'I do my best.' Barry returned the favour with his own gappy beam. Ms McCann looked up at the clock on the wall to see both hands travelling even quicker but in the same direction. 'Okay, Mr Harris, it's almost time for your departure, I'll be back with a map you'll need to follow. Feel free to use the services while you are waiting.'

'Just one last thing, you don't happen to have a chemist here do you?'

'No, this isn't an airport you know! What is it you need?'

'Never mind, nothing, it doesn't matter.'

With all this excitement, Barry's entrails were making the kind of noise that results from stealing a juicy bone from a grumpy basset hound. He thought it prudent to go and find out what an intergalactic lavatory looked like.

Wandering around, he arrived at a spiral staircase and a sign reading, "Departure Lounge This Way". Barry clambered up the rusty jangling steps to find himself in an immense glass-domed atrium. It was the most spectacular thing he had ever seen. It looked like the whole universe lay before him, shooting stars were disappearing into black holes as tubes siphoned people in all directions. Spacecraft of all shapes and sizes lit up the horizon. *I wish mum and Mindy could be here to see this!* thought Barry. *Who is ever going to believe me when I tell them?* Staring into infinity he marvelled at the countless beings surrounding him. A reflection that would ordinarily have made him feel utterly insignificant. Today however, he smiled to himself, as at last he felt part of this vast unfathomable cosmic game.

Continuing his search, he walked down a dimly lit corridor, arriving at a door that was simply marked X. Poking his head inside, he could see rows of shiny silver cubicles. *There must be a lot of staff here,* thought Barry as he rushed into one and sat down on what looked like a glass bucket. As he began emptying his underwear, he could hear a loud gurgling noise. He presumed it must have been the kebab he had devoured earlier.

Looking down, he could see a small whirlpool emerging from the bottom of the bowl which was getting faster and faster. A fierce suction started drawing Barry downward and he desperately gripped the sides of the toilet to stop himself being dragged in.

'Help!' yelped Barry, holding on with all his might. A loud voice honked from the tannoy.

'Welcome, traveller. You are now entering the Time Vortex Translocation System. We hope you have a pleasant journey.' Two large hands reached out of the middle of the whirlpool and grabbed hold of Barry's buttocks, yanking him down into the torrent below.

His pants still around his ankles, Barry emerged, unceremoniously flushed into a huge heap of green slime. Poking his head from the slime, there appeared to be nothing but desert surrounding him. The sky was a sepia haze, with no sun to be seen, just a weird twilight. Standing over him was a small being, no more than three feet, with no eyes, ears or nose. It had spindly looping arms that were twice the size of its body. Barry blinked a few times to confirm to himself that he was actually seeing what he was seeing.

Helping him out of the slime, the being spoke.

'Hello I'm Armitage Frank. I guide people between worlds. Can you show me your map please?'

'Where am I?'

'You are in The Before and After.'

'How can you hear me without any ears?' asked Barry, scraping the slime from himself.

'I spend my life pulling people through time-toilets. I have only one orifice for all my bodily functions. It's much more practical.'

'Only one?...even for... never mind. I left before I could get a map...by accident, actually.'

'You what? You can't be in The Before and After without a map – you could get lost for all eternity. I've had four-hundred-and-twenty cats, eighty-five dogs and twelve guinea pigs go missing down here. You never age, you just walk round and round in circles. Forever. I'm worried they will all come back and find me on the same day! You must have a map.'

'Do I have to go back up into that toilet?'

'That's the only way in and out.'

'Bugger that. I'll take my chances. Can you just explain to me roughly where to go?'

'Who knows? In this place somewhere is nowhere and nowhere is everywhere.'

'Great! I won't ask to borrow an A-to-Z then. What happens if I go that way?' Barry pointed to what he thought might be north.

'No, no. Never ever go that way. That takes you through The Forest of Unattainable Dreams and Ghastly Consequences.'

'What happens there?'

'You can never get what you want and if you get upset about it you're severely punished.'

'What about if I go south then?' Barry made a guess and pointed.

'There is no magnetic field in The Before and After so how do you know which way is south?' Frank then pointed in what seemed to be the same direction as Barry. 'If you mean that way, you mustn't go that way! There you find The Forest of Fabulous Abundance and Pitiful Remorse. There you can fulfil your hearts desires, have anything you want, but only with debilitating regret for the rest of your days.'

'What the hell is this place?' Barry got up and started pacing up and down on the coarse desert sand, 'Please just tell me the way to Japan?' Frank pointed wildly in another random direction.

'That way takes you to The Sea of Non-dual Materialism.'

'What?'

'Trust me, you don't want to go there. Your only hope is to walk into the prevailing wind, which takes you deeper into

The Desert of Existential Mirrors, where nothing exists but everything is possible. Be careful, a sandstorm is brewing.'

Wrapping his t-shirt around his face, Barry set off into the gritty, cutting wind. It was slow going with his head down, the diamond dust coating his skin. A coppery tang registered at the back of his mouth and a fuzzy background tinnitus ricocheted in the wind like a poorly tuned radio station. He tried desperately to walk in some sort of straight line, fearing the price of going off-piste. After miles upon miles of arid wasteland, he could walk no more. Deliriously tired, it was all he could do to curl up into the sand and fall fast asleep.

He quickly found himself back in his night terror, though this time it was him standing on the cliff, and his father hanging from the edge. Barry reached down for his father's hand but Yamoshi knocked it away.

'You have to go back home Barry, it's too dangerous for you here.' With that Yamoshi let go and sent himself hurtling to the rocks below.

Barry awoke, gasping wildly for breath, almost fully covered in sand. The wind had given way to a ghostly calm and the only sounds were a kettle of vultures circling above him. *Didn't Frank say nothing existed here?*

As soon as he had collected himself, Barry jumped to his feet and set off into nowhere again as the last of the light evaporated. Faint from not having eaten anything since leaving Portslade, he wasn't sure how much longer he would last. The cabaret of night began fabricating faces in the distance, seemingly familiar but disappearing before he could place them. He sensed he was being followed but didn't have the strength to walk any faster. A cacophony of tiny voices behind him competed with the desert hum.

'There he is, the little bastard. I told you we'd find him.'

'There's no sense running, Mister. You'll never escape us.'

Barry turned round to see gangs of garden gnomes surrounding him, tooled up with little knives and crowbars.

'This will teach you for deserting us!' The gnomes swarmed up his legs, dragging him to the ground and sticking their little weapons into him.

Barry picked one of the gnomes up and used him to smash the rest of them. But as soon as one went down two more appeared, flooding in from all directions. Slowly drowning in psycho gnomes, Barry saw a dark figure approaching him. Squinting to try to make out who or what it was, a white cowboy hat emerged... followed by a bright blue suit with a gun hanging from its hip in its holster. As the figure got closer, he saw his iconic black mask.

'Oh fuck me, it's The Lone Ranger! I know what this is! My mind is regurgitating itself into this place. Like a weird dream. '

The realisation instantly dismantled Barry's tiny tormentors, who started turning to dust. The Lone Ranger smiled, tipped his hat and walked back into the night.

Lying alone, exhausted on the desert floor, Barry had not an inkling of what to do next. *Will I be lost in this place for all eternity, inside the bizarre theatre of my own mind? That's the closest vision of hell I can think of.*

The rumination was interrupted as words appeared in front of him, painted onto the black canvas of The Before and After:

Forget everything you think you know, catch the sun and make it snow.

. . .

It was the koan his father had given him all those years earlier, that Barry had so passionately sought to decipher but had always drawn a blank. Now they seemed a little different; the words were more alive in some way, more accessible. It was as if they were inviting him to a secret conversation, a glimpse of something sacred, calling him, waiting for him. Then it occurred to Barry, *if I can make things disappear, surely I can make this place anything I want. Can't I?* He sat up, closed his eyes and meditated.

Watching his breath to calm himself, he visualised a torii, the symbolic Japanese gateway that marks the entrance to a temple. With its large wooden posts and imposing bowed top beam, Barry held the image in his mind, sitting for what felt like hours upon hours, until he could sit no more.

He opened his eyes. Before him was a vast wooden gateway, the number 1603 inscribed upon it. He stepped inside and disappeared.

Chapter Eight

1603

Barry found himself upon a misty hilltop in front of the most intoxicating vista he had ever witnessed. Antique woodlands conspired on curvaceous hilltops and cornflowers lined meadows in the valley below. A deep indigo sky merged perfectly with the surrounding ocean as black crane birds hovered on the gentle sea breeze. Had he really gone back in time? Was this ancient Japan? There was a sharp frost in the air, infused by the sweet smell of burning pine from a nearby fire. It was a good job his new surroundings were aromatic as his underwear were really starting to show the strain. He was slowing turning into a walking compost heap.

There was the sound of a commotion coming from a nearby forest and Barry decided he should investigate. He knelt down by a small pond and smeared mud over his face and arms to blend in with his environment – maximum stealth mode. Staying away from the path, he crept silently through the trees toward a clearing up ahead.

As the noise got louder, he crouched behind a bush and saw that two samurai soldiers were taunting and pushing an old man on the dusty forest path.

Watching this unfold, Barry became acutely aware of how differently he felt now. Where fear would be normally be crippling him, he felt determination. Instead of paralysing anxiety and doubt, he felt purpose. Without thinking, Barry jumped into the clearing and shrieked,

'You bastards! Come and do that to me if you think you can handle it!'

The samurai stopped what they were doing, looked at Barry, looked at each other, and burst out laughing.

'How fucking dare you,' growled Barry. 'I've just travelled four-hundred-and-thirty-six years back in time, and I'm going to kick your arse!' Running straight at the first samurai, he disarmed him by flinging a handful of coarse sand and cayenne pepper directly into his eyes – a ninja trick called "Metsubishi-Ko". The Samurai fell to his knees, clutching desperately at his face as Barry stole his sword and sliced him through the back. He fell to the floor in two pieces. The remaining soldier drew his sword and held it in front of him, wobbling like a jelly and custard pudding.

'You seem to have stopped laughing – am I not funny anymore?' Barry jumped up, kicked the sword out of the soldier's hands, and launched into hand-to-hand combat. He had never felt more alive. Everything his father had taught him seemed to be falling into place. Grabbing the arm of the soldier, Barry threw him over his shoulder and face-first into the side of a tree. He slid down the tree and hit the forest floor like a sack of parsnips.

Barry walked over and helped the elderly man to his feet.

'Are you okay?'

'I am, thank you. You have skills, young man. Tell me, where do you come from?'

'Portslade.' Barry began picking up the man's scattered belongings.

'Where is this kingdom you speak of?'

'It's between Aldrington and Hove on the south coast of England.'

'Hmm, you are far, far from home.'

'I have been sent here to find my father and fulfil a prophecy.'

'Hmm, I think it would be wise to take you to meet the village elders; their council will direct you.' The old man stroked his leathery chin, then pushed down on his walking stick to set himself in motion.

As they disappeared into the forest, Barry reflected on the fight. He couldn't quite believe that it was him in action back there. He knew all those techniques, but only as pictures in his head, he thought. When the fight was on, the moves had seemed to pour from his soul.

'So what's your name?' asked Barry, moving closer to the old man who was carefully navigating the rough terrain.

'I am Haruki.'

'Have you lived here long?'

'It has been so very long that I can't remember if I moved here yesterday.' Barry twisted his head sideways as if to make sense of it from another perspective.

'OK, what time will we arrive?'

'When you arrive, you will know. How can it be any other way?' After many more hours of walking, they arrived at a glade that was home to a spectacular wooden temple. It was identical to the one in the picture his father had given him. *This is it,* thought Barry. *This is exactly where I need to be.*

They were greeted at the temple door by a man dressed head to foot in black. *Oh my god, a real life ninja!* Barry could hardly contain himself as he was ushered in and led to a dining hall with five older men sat around a table drinking tea.

'Please take a seat over here and drink some tea. I will speak to the council and return soon.' Haruki wandered over to the other men and was soon engaged in what looked like an animated discussion.

An hour passed. Barry was tired and hungry. There's only so long you can sit comfortably on a rice mat, even if you do have the benefits of 15 tog quilted underwear.

Eventually Haruki shuffled back to Barry.

'I have been talking with the wise elders and telling them about your quest. They would like to know why you have shit on your face?'

'What? It took you an hour to come up with that? It's not shit, it's mud. I was using my ninja training to keep undercover so I could rescue you.' With that, Haruki sauntered back to the council. Barry felt his stomach moan. Sweat beads grew and ran down the side of his face. A faint flicker on the edge of his lip began to reassert itself. *What kind of fucking wise council is this? Laurel and Hardy could do a better job!* Another long hour passed before Haruki returned.

'It is clear you have talents, young man, but talk of the prophecy is premature. The council say you need to prove yourself a true ninja before they can help you with your quest. For this you need to complete the five sacred tasks.'

'Okay. What are they?' Barry stood up, trying look prepared.

Haruki shuffled close to Barry, his eyes wide and as his eyebrows seemingly ready to leave his forehead.

'Young man, to prove yourself, you must:
   1) Run faster than a cheetah
   2) Mimic the song of the Japanese bush warbler
   3) Wrestle a goat
   4) Strangle a baboon

5) Put a donkey in a headlock.'

'They're a bit random, aren't they?' asked Barry.

'From time immemorial, it has been this way.'

'Look, I don't want to cause a fuss. I just want to rescue my father. His name is Yamochi Harris. I've been told he's being held hostage by a warlord. Do you know him?'

The look on the old man's face became even more animated, and he jumped back into conversation with the elders.

This time, after only a few moments, the elders shuffled across the room toward Barry in unison.

A petite, withered elder stepped out of the group and snatched his hand.

'Young man, this is indeed an auspicious meeting. Yamochi, your father, is the leader of our ninja army. He was the first of us to stand up and defend the poor. Most of our fighters are simple farming folk who have had to learn their skills quickly. We fight bravely but we are outnumbered, and few of us are now left. The evil warlord Nobmearda you speak of ambushed this temple and kidnapped your father. We don't know if Yamochi is still alive. If he is, he will be under the spell of a dark wizard who, in league with Nobmeada, is summoning eighty-thousand samurai warriors to Rim province. So is it rumoured. This is a critical time for the ninja community; if we lose your father, we lose everything.'

'I've come a long way and waited a long time. I'm not going to let anything happen to my father now. Take me to where he is being held captive.'

'Eat and rest. At first light you go.'

. . .

However much he needed both those things, Barry had to sort his underwear out. He borrowed a knife from the kitchen and cut himself a small section of rice matting which he used as a temporary gusset repair kit. Barry hoped this might buy him a bit of extra bum support time, though he knew the clock was ticking.

Later that evening, the elders regaled him with stories about his father's incredible adventures and unsurpassed abilities. They were all keen to know if Barry had inherited his father's gifts. When asked, Barry shrugged and said.

'We'll soon find out, won't we?'

Eventually, lying down to rest, Barry thought about everyone back in Portslade and what they would make of all this. *I could do with Mum and Merril out here.* He smiled. *They'd give the samurai a run for their money.*

Barry was brusquely awoken at five the next morning by the mysterious ninja from the day before. Saying nothing, the ninja gestured at the door and disappeared through it.

Splashing some icy water into his face, Barry said goodbye to the temple and chased after his guide. Travelling light and fast, they were soon traversing a steep forested hill, as first light crept in through the tree canopy. The anticipation was growing for Barry with every step he took toward finding his father. He also thought it was pretty cool to spend some time with a real life ninja.

'How long have you been a ninja then?'

No response.

'I like your nunchucks. Where did you buy them? I've not seen any shops anywhere.'

No response.

'So what kind of music are you into?' Barry was puffing as they approached the brow of the hill.

No response.

'What do you get up to on the weekends?'

Nothing

Barry looked up to admire the crimson glare of the rising sun through the misty morning cobwebs.

'I'm the only ninja in England that I know of.'

The ninja turned to Barry and pointed into the valley below.

'You are not a ninja and that is where your father is.' He pointed toward a vast temple complex surrounded by a moat and hundreds of guards. Above the temple was a cliff line and a deep blue ocean stretching beyond it toward the horizon. It was savagely beautiful. White wisteria blossoms clambered up the steep temple walls as the morning mist evaporated into the forest above. Red maple trees lined the valley pathways and Japanese nightingales harmonised with distant wind chimes. The chatty ninja turned his back and disappeared down the hill.

'Lovely spending time with you! We must do this again sometime!' shouted Barry after him.

Alone, he sat down on the hilltop and took in the cold reality of his mission impossible. *How the hell am I gonna get into that place? There must be five hundred samurai surrounding it.* His excitement evaporated and anxiety crept back in. Queasiness was accompanied by an all-too-familiar deep intestinal rumbling. *What if I don't succeed? What will happen to Dad? How will Mum cope if I never return?*

He made his way down the hill into the valley and hid in the tree line, hoping to find some inspiration to hatch a rudimentary plan. There were around twenty encampments surrounding the temple moat, each with its own log fire and division of soldiers. It appeared that most of the samurai were still asleep, with only one soldier keeping watch. If Barry could sneak through the long grass between two of these camps, he might just make it to the moat.

Putting on his ninja head mask, he sank into the misty meadow grass and wriggled towards the encampments. This had to be the ultimate stealth operation. Nothing that Barry had previously attempted had stakes as high as this. He had to be quieter than an amoeba holding its breath and sleeker than a panther in a Versace suit. Unfortunately, with all the excitement his innards were bubbling like an insane witch's broth. Barry tightened his belt as far as it would go hoping to pacify the demonic intestinal lord that did torture him so.

He successfully inched his way past the first camp. Through the sweat in his eyes he could see two more camps up ahead, each with their own guard slumped by an open fire. There must have been only five metres between them. If Barry could get through this gap he would have a clear run to the moat. His heart hammered against his rib cage but his breath was faint a whisper as he crept forward.

Drawing parallel with the guards, he paused. He could see the moat ahead. *If I get up and run for it I can be in the moat before they realise what's going on,* thought Barry, not knowing what his best move was. One of the guards stood up and walked in his direction so he lay flat on the grass hoping he wouldn't be seen. The guard stopped some two metres away and relieved himself. Panic had aggravated Barry's bowels to such a degree that they were now rumbling like a magnitude six earthquake. *Can he hear me? He could spear me from where he is and I wouldn't stand a chance. I've got to run!*

Barry jumped to his feet with such fury that his belt snapped, and as it did he let rip the most earth-shattering passing of wind he had ever known. It was a noise so harrowing and awesome that not only did it almost give the unsuspecting guard a heart attack but it also woke the rest of the sleeping samurai. It could quite possibly have woken the dead.

Shouts from the guards rang out.

'Ninja! Ninja attack! Bring your weapons!'

Unsure if he had soiled himself, Barry had no choice but to double back to the tree line. He could hear the samurai gaining on him. Had they known what they were getting into, they may well have kept their distance.

Barry made it into the forest and scrambled up the first tree he could find. He only just made it onto the horizontal limb of a dense pine branch. Looking down, he could see the samurai entering the forest and gathering around the base of his tree. Lying as still as the temple walls, he could hear orders being given out as warriors dispersed in all directions in search of him. *They haven't seen me, I'll hide out here until nightfall, then make my next move.*

No sooner had Barry finished his thought than a loud cracking noise echoed through the forest. The branch he was on decided it would snap beneath his weight and toss him ruthlessly to the wolves below.

Chapter Nine

HORNY WIZARD APOCALYPSE

A n excruciating pain tore though Barry's body. He had awoken to find himself strapped to a tree in one of the samurai camps. He linked his foot round the branch of a nearby shrub to try and get free but couldn't move and inch. *I think I've broken my fucking arm.*

A gang of soldiers sat around a fire some ten metres away. They stared at him and smiled while they sharpened their swords. New battalions of samurai were emerging from the surrounding forest. Out of the throng of warriors appeared Robbie in a bright gold cape with his hair back-combed vertically into a large fan shape, looking like a cosmic peacock.

'Hey, baby. What's cooking? Long time no see.'

'It's only been about four hundred years. I could wait longer if I'm honest,' replied Barry.

'You're a gas baby, and by the smell of it that's exactly what you're producing! I should have wiped you out a long time ago. Don't worry though. As soon as master Nobmearda arrives, I'll be making up for lost time. This was one spectacle the master wouldn't want to miss – I couldn't have planned it better myself. If you're lucky, they might bring your dad to come and watch the show too!' Robbie turned, fanning his cape in the wind and disappearing into the samurai, singing to himself, 'The end is near... so I face the final curtain... ha ha ha!'

So this is how it ends! I've come all this way just to be a sitting duck for a twisted wizard and an insane warlord.

At least Barry finally knew why his father had gone missing. Despite the burden of guilt he had carried all these years, it wasn't his fault after all. Scant consolation for what was about to happen, though. He could see a procession coming out of the temple and crossing the moat bridge towards his encampment. A tall man in white robes was surrounded by samurai in black gowns and steel-plated armour. These soldiers seemed much taller than the rest; they were obviously some kind of elite guard. Out in front was a man being pushed forward with his hands tied in front of him.

Is that... my god... It's Dad! Yamochi had his head down and was staring at the floor. Barry's heart raced. He clawed at his ropes so fiercely his nails started to bleed.

The samurai surrounding Barry left to go and pay their respects to their arriving warlord; three bows followed by a prostration that symbolised the soldier's devotion to their master. *It's hardly any wonder these warlords become such arseholes.* Barry closed his eyes. He tried to pretend this wasn't really happening. As he sat in self-imposed blindness, a faint voice began whispering behind him.

'Alright, geezer?'

'Terry! Thank god! Where are you?'

'Shh, put a sock in it, I've got a Jackie Chan innit! I'm going to shuffle over behind you, undo that rope and when I do, jump in this shrub with me and we'll do a runner.'

Barry could feel a rustling behind him as his tethers fell away. He hopped into the shrub to see a small man wearing only underpants and a pair of wellington boots. Barry couldn't take his eyes off him.

'I never thought you would just be a bloke in a bush. I thought you were some kind of ethereal being.'

'I am, kind of, it's difficult to explain. I'm taking human form so you don't get too freaked out when you look at me.'

'It's working so far, but why couldn't you just show up in a robe like Obi-Wan Kenobi?'

'I wanted to but my boss wouldn't let me, it's all USP's these days innit? Anyway, we better scarper. We only got ten minutes. The hoops I had jump to get a time extension beggars belief.' They shuffled towards a group of trees next to the castle moat.

'Right, we should be safe here for a while.' Terry reached into the back of the bush and pulled out a canvas bag.

'I put this bag together with everything you'll need to complete your mission: a flute, toothpicks, waxed rope, poisonous berries, some aftershave and a wireless in-ear-canal earpiece.'

'Toothpicks? Don't you think some dynamite might have been a bit more useful?'

'Too noisy. Remember, Barry, "the best ninja has no smell, leaves no name and makes everyone wonder if he ever existed." I suggest you meditate before going into battle, all good ninjas do that. By the way, you better use the earpiece to check-in with head office before you get started. You might wanna have a flutter with the aftershave too, smells like something's well Pete Tong with your khyber.' Having imparted that transcendental wisdom, a bright green flash filled the bush, and Barry was alone again.

Picking his way through the bag, Barry wondered what the hell he was going to do with this bizarre bunch of objects. As his arm was in agony, he used some of the rope to make himself a mock-sling. Not only was he going to have to complete the mission against impossible odds, he was going to have to do it with one arm. Reflecting on the advice Terry had given him, he decided to stay true to ninjutsu tradition and meditate. In fact, he vowed to not move until he was completely ready for battle.

He sat, unflinching through the searing tyrannical pain in his arm. It was like barbed wire being pulled through his veins, but he did not move. Tears surged down his cheeks. He could hear the samurai searching through the undergrowth for him. He sat perfectly still. Barry brought to mind a mantra his father used to say to him whenever he had hurt himself:

This pain is not me; it is not mine.

Barry repeated it inwardly over and over as intoxicating images filled his mind. A mirage of Madam Zanzibar danced naked before him, beckoning him.

'Come, be with me, Barry. Leave this foolish quest behind.'

Barry continued with his meditation, focusing on his abdomen rising and falling, rising and falling. Just when Barry thought his agony couldn't get any worse, Robbie popped into this waking nightmare, gyrating like a belly dancer, wearing only his cape and a leopard-skin thong.

'You can't be far, Barry. I will find you and when I do, I will tear you into a thousand pieces. Ha ha ha!'

Perfectly poised, Barry maintained his mindfulness as Robbie's evil laugh evaporated into the afternoon breeze. But the pain was building to a crescendo; Barry's vision was blurring, delirium was taking hold. Jolts of energy erupted in his body, each one a pocket-sized exploding star. A volcanic fever shot through him and lava filled his head.

Just when he thought he could take no more... bam!

Blinding light swallowed him, his body felt like it had been blown into a billion pieces, with only his spirit left, cradled by the sun. It was bliss. Pain, worry and fear fell away, as if he had found the missing piece to a jigsaw puzzle he had been searching for all his life. Sitting in this new found joy, he knew it was now time to act. He reached into his bag and pulled out the earpiece.

'Good afternoon Mr Harris and welcome to The Ninja Prophecy, number 231/129.4. I'm Chantel and I'll be your personal navigational support assistant today. Here at the Prophecy Allocation Department we understand that a mission of this kind can seem a little daunting when you are first starting out.'

'You could say that,' replied Barry.

'That's why we recommend you take advantage of our Premium Guardianship Service which is on special offer at only £500,000.'

'No problem, that'll only take me around a hundred life-times to pay off.'

'Future life financial schemes are available as part of our service package you'll be pleased to know. With this offer you will have ongoing support from the prophecy allocation team virtual simulation predictor. Our algorithms can analyse data from thousands of similar missions to enable us to accurately predict your best options as you proceed through your mission.'

'Oh what the hell, ok, I need all the help I can get!'

'We think that is a wise choice. To get you started we recommend you break your mission into a three-phase approach. Studies have shown that giving yourself achievable aims improves your chances of success by 8% as well as any associated risks to your self-esteem and/or loss of life.'

'That's encouraging.'

'We wish you the best of luck, and remember, you only

need to ask should you need support.'

Phase One - The Barracks

Poking his head out of the bush, Barry saw that night had descended. He picked up his bag and made his way down to the muddy edge of the moat. It suddenly occurred to him that this might be the perfect opportunity to ditch his underwear. At this stage of the proceedings it was a bit misleading even to call them underwear; they were more like an underground bunker built for the long term storage of nuclear waste. Just as he had dropped his underwear round his ankles Barry felt a presence. He looked up and saw an elite samurai guard. Turning to run, he tripped on his pants and fell face-first into the mud. The samurai drew his sword and ran down the bank toward him. As he was about to strike, Barry's silent ninja guide leaped from the top of the bank and sent the samurai reeling backward. Jumping onto the guard, the ninja plunged a dagger deep into his chest. As he did so, the samurai impaled him on his sword, returning the favour. Stepping away from the dead samurai, the ninja fell to his knees, clutching his stomach. Barry secured his underwear and ran over. Blood was oozing from the ninja's mouth.

'I'm sorry I doubted your bravery,' gasped the ninja, 'keep going...never give up!'

Handing Barry a small canvas pouch, he whispered, 'Take these herbs...they will help you.'

The ninja's eyes closed, and his body went limp. Fearing more soldiers would come, Barry pocketed the pouch and submerged himself in the freezing water. Using the flute to poke above the surface and breathe, he worked his way through the thick marsh reeds. He had almost turned blue by the time he reached the other side. Trying to steady his shaking hands, he scaled the bank beneath the steep temple walls.

Barry then tied the rope between his ankles, enabling him to a scale a tree adjacent to the temple wall. As he climbed higher, he could see neither movement nor sound coming from the temple grounds. *Everyone must be asleep. Any guards awake? Where will they be keeping Dad?*

Barry was now high enough to see into the temple forecourt. A barracks housing the samurai foot soldiers lay in front of a vast cylindrical brick tower. *He must be in that tower; it's the most secure place. How am I going to get in through those barracks?* Barry pulled on his ninja mask and jumped from the treetop onto the top of the temple wall.

Sliding down the rope into the temple grounds, he moved like a ghost in the wind, making his way through the white gravel courtyard to the entrance of the barracks. No sign of life anywhere. Sliding open the Shōji paper doors, his heart sank when he saw hundreds of samurai asleep on the floor. The narrow entrance to the tower was at the far end of the room. Would he be able to get through those sleeping soldiers unheard? He crept back into the courtyard and, inserting his earpiece, whispered,

'Chantel, I'm in a situation here. Is there any way I can get to the tower without going through the barracks?'

'No.'

'What?'

'No.'

'I'm paying half-a-million quid and all you give me is a no?'

'Our 3D virtual mapping and risk analysis system calculates you have a 3% chance of survival going through the barracks, but only a 2% chance if you attempt to climb over the roof and up the outside of the tower.' Barry shook his head, tutted and headed back to the Shōji doors. Entering slowly, Barry placed his foot down carefully onto the rice straw matting and stepped over the first soldier – one foot out of place would be fatal. He moved in the direction of a snoring samurai hoping to muffle any sound he made.

Creeping gently over the slumbering warriors, Barry's eyes were frantically trying to map the positions of the deadly silhouettes before him. A drip of sweat fell from his head but he managed to reach down and catch it before it hit the matting. A soldier turned in his sleep in front of Barry and he almost lost his footing. He paused to centre himself and saw he had made it halfway across the room. *Almost there. Keep going. You can do this.* He lifted his leg to step over another soldier when a hand reached out and grabbed Barry's ankle.

'Invader!' came a cry. It was like Barry had been dropped into a pond as the soldiers rippled from slumber around him. He drop-kicked the samurai who had grabbed him and ran like a hurricane toward the entrance of the tower. He ran on top of the samurai now, to keep them pinned the floor and to prevent them from blocking his path – a sharp ploy that got him all the way to the tower unscathed.

Phase Two - The Tower

On entering the doorway Barry noticed two large bookcases on either side. He jumped and pulled them down, blocking the entrance behind him. Sprinting up the narrow staircase, he arrived at the first landing. Two large elite samurai stood before him like animated gargoyles. They drew their swords, slicing the air as they approached him.

'Hello Chantel, me again. I definitely need some fucking help now!'

'Yes Mr Harris, I believe you do. Our algorithms calculate

you have 0.2% probability of surviving this interaction. Please look in your bag for your gun, this should help you.'

'A gun? There's no gun, there's some fucking tooth picks but no gun!'

'Did he put deodorant in by any chance?'

'Yes.'

'I'm awfully sorry Mr Harris, we have disciplined Terry about this before. He's very old fashioned you see and believes ninjas shouldn't rely on any form of modern technology. I'm afraid there's nothing else we can do, but please rest assured I will have stern words with him.'

'Shitting heck! Remind me to never trust a fucking hedge again!' Barry desperately scrambled through his bag and, without thinking, took out his flute and played the only song he knew: "Trust In Me" from *The Jungle Book*. Molly had taught it to him on his fifth birthday. Barry then started singing to them.

'Trust in me... just in me... shut your eyes... trust in me

You can sleep safe and sound... knowing I am around.'

The guards looked perplexed, not knowing how to react, as the song weaved its hypnotic spell they became sluggish, losing their coordination. One dropped his sword while the other began a slow dance with himself.

By the time Barry had finished, they were both fast asleep spooning each other on the floor. *Close call,* thought Barry, continuing up the tower.

Phase Three - The Horny Wizard

The higher he got the narrower the passage became until the skin from his arms was being scraped off by the rough stone walls.

Dragging himself up the final staircase, he reached the top floor of the tower and found himself in a small empty room with no windows and a large wooden door at one end. The door was adorned with dazzling jewels that formed a five-pointed star. Barry could hear the samurai climbing up the tower toward him. He ran over to the door and tried to push it open.

'Is anyone in there?'

'Barry! I've so longed to hear your voice, my son.'

'Dad! I've come to save you!'

'Barry, please save yourself. There are too many to fight and the wizard is too strong. He has cast some kind of spell on me; my powers aren't working!'

'How can we lift the spell?'

'Only by killing the wizard, but it's too dangerous!'

'You taught me never to run, dad, I'm not going to start now. Where do they keep the key to this door?' With that question, Barry was whisked off the ground, and thrust up against the ceiling by an invisible force. Robbie materialised out of nowhere, billowing his arms as if conducting an orchestra.

'Chantel! Me again, I'm currently being held against the ceiling of the tower by a wizard in a leopard-skin thong. Anything you can offer me?'

'Hello Mr Harris, unfortunately our policy doesn't cover wizards, dragons or aliens and I'm on my lunch break.'

'Great, that was the best half-a-mil I've ever spent.' Barry looked down at Robbie.

'You haven't got time to give me a quick haircut have you?'

'Hey, baby! I'm afraid not but I do have something you might be interested in. The key to that door, it's tied to my thong, why don't you come get it?' Wiping the sweat from his forehead, Robbie clicked his fingers, sending Barry crashing to the ground. Barry jumped to his feet and ran towards

Robbie like a banshee on fire, but with a simple wafting gesture Robbie hurled him back across the room.

'It's show time! Are you ready for the main event, Barry? I've been so looking forward to this!' Robbie threw his cape over his shoulder and made a frenzied display of arcane shapes with his hands. Then thrusting them high in the air, he chanted an incantation.

'I call upon Sambō-Kōjin the goddess of fire. Grant me your wrath so I can burn this pestilence from the world.' Trickling streams of burning liquid oozed from Robbie's hands, forming a web of fire.

'Yabaam!' He hurled it at Barry, who dodged it by diving sideward just in time. As he hit the floor his earpiece flew out and smashed into pieces against the wall. The burning web stuck to the ceiling and set the rafters ablaze.

'That was just a warm up.' Robbie laughed, preparing a huge fireball.

Barry got up and put his back against the door of his father's prison cell. The ascending samurai were almost upon them. *How the hell am I going to get out of this?*

Robbie raised the pulsating fireball and launched it at Barry.

His fate all but sealed, a familiar whisper came through the door. 'Remember what I taught you, Barry; forget everything you think you know. If you believe you are invisible, you will become invisible!'

Barry closed his eyes and returned to when he was six, sitting on the carpet in his front room, his dad's soft brown eyes studying him. He could feel his father's love and unwavering belief flooding into him, but an explosion dragged him back to the burning tower. Through the falling bricks and smoke, he could see Robbie looking around the room for him.

'Hey, brother. I hope you haven't left the party. You haven't seen the main event yet.'

Barry realised Robbie couldn't see him. It had worked! Running over to the corner of the room, he reached into his bag, took out the toothpicks and turned them into poison tipped darts by pushing them into the berries that Terry had given him.

'Where are you, you little ant? I'm going to crush you!' As Robbie's frustration grew, lightening and fireballs erupted from him. Huge chunks of wall imploded as the fire spreading throughout the roof raged above them.

Filling up his flute with the toothpicks, Barry blew with all his might. Robbie let out a shriek as one hit him in the side of the neck. He reached out, gasping for breath, grabbing wildly at the wall to steady himself. His face turned a sickening ash as he gripped his throat. Barry grabbed the keys from Robbie's thong and, struck with a sudden inspiration, unfastened the velcro straps to his underwear.

Robbie's eyes filled with terror as Barry whipped his underwear off and pulled the toxic mother-load firmly over Robbie's head. Barry held on for all he was worth as Robbie bashed against the walls, choking on a delicious blend of partly-digested fish-fingers and radioactive rice matt. Robbie made a gurgling noise as Barry pushed him towards the top of the staircase. Robbie's hands fell to his sides. A feeble whisper came from within the fermenting underwear.

'Help me...please.'

'Help you? Sure thing mate, I'll help you.' Barry jumped high into the air and kicked Robbie with all his remaining strength. The wizard went flailing down the stairs onto the arriving samurai.

'I'll help you to stop being such a motherfucker!'

Barry pushed the key under the big wooden door.

'Dad, the soldiers are coming. Stay in there for now. I'm

going to distract them.' As the first samurai scrambled over Robbie's writhing body, Barry found a hole in the wall.

'Come and get me, losers!' Barry dived from the top of the burning tower into the moat a hundred metres below.

As Barry landed in the moat, the samurai lining the banks began throwing their razor sharp yari spears. One found its mark, taking a chunk out of the side of Barry's leg. Ducking under the water, he swam through the reeds, following the moat to the back of the temple where he crawled out and made it to the tree line.

The soldiers were hot on his heels, arrows whistling past his ears. Barry just kept running.

Entering the forest, he scrambled up a steep incline. Pine needles pierced his skin, the pain from his arm intensified, and blood poured from his leg. But he didn't stop. Gritting his teeth, he drove himself onward and upward toward the peak. Arrows were hitting the trees all around him; the samurai were gaining ground.

Reaching the top, Barry stepped forward to find himself peering over a high cliff-edge. The waves below smashed against knife-edged rocks. *How could I survive that?*

Before he had the chance to think anything else, he felt a sharp thud as an arrow tore into his shoulder. It threw him forwards and, slipping on the gravel, he fell. Hurtling downward, Barry grabbed desperately for any outcrop of rock. Finding one, he brought his body smashing into the flint rock face. Unable to keep his grip, he slid further down and hit an old tree root that he managed to cling to. Dangling in the sea air, a samurai approached the ledge above him and delicately drew his sword. He knew this most desired of prizes could elevate him to greatness in his master's eyes.

This is it, thought Barry, *the moment from my dreams. It's what I've been preparing for my whole life. This is where I prove myself.*

The soldier edged closer as the root gradually dislodged itself from its fastening. Hanging by a thread, his death only seconds away, Barry closed his eyes and travelled inward once again, watching his breath rising and falling, in harmony with the waves below. Bliss rose up and found him again. The widest of smiles swept across his face. The kind of smile Molly has at a Slayer concert.

Yes, of course. I know the answer – I've known it all along. With that, Barry let go, falling to the rocks below. He looked up at the sun, its rays focused into a single beam that hit him between the eyes. Reality blurred and whirled like an old kaleidoscope. Things became quieter and quieter until the sound of silence rang out, and just for a moment, the world vanished.

Floating in an unknown darkness, a frosty sensation swept over him. Holding his arm up close, he watched as it turned a bright glowing white. Brimming with ecstasy, he called out, 'Look! It's true. I can make it snow!'

Sparks lit up the horizon as thick white marshmallows fell from the sky, filling up the ocean. Barry fell through the wet foggy haze, shudders reverberated down his spine as he landed in his ice cream miracle.

He looked up to see the shards of sun penetrating the falling snow. The blurred outline of a figure reached down, took his hand, and pulled him toward the surface.

Wiping the snow from his eyes, he saw his father's smiling face.

Yamoshi wrapped him in a blanket and sat in front of him. Though his face was older, the same brown eyes fell upon Barry.

'My son, how happy I am... you... are a true ninja.'

Chapter Ten

BACK TO THE FUCHSIA

Putting on her favourite Napalm Death album, Molly sat down at the kitchen table with her family for the first time in twenty-five years.

'I never thought this day would come. I'm so happy.' She blew her nose on an outrageously snotty tissue.

'You should have seen Robbie freak out when I became invisible, Mum!'

'Ha ha! What a cock.' Molly passed around a packet of custard creams.

'You should have seen the commotion round here went you both went missing. No one could give us any answers. We were like two rabid dogs at the police station.' Molly stood up and wrapped her arms tenderly around her husband.

'Do you know, my darling, the inspector leading the investigation had the nerve to suggest you were shagging a Japanese glamour model. They found a photograph in your underwear drawer.'

'That's slander...she was...helping me...with some enquiries...related to the ninja resistance,' spluttered Yamochi with a face you could fry an egg on.

'We've not finished talking about that.' Molly folded her arms and walked back across the kitchen. Barry jumped to his father's aid.

'So how come you didn't tell us why you were leaving, Dad? Why was everything so cryptic?'

'That was all part of your training, Barry. Without it, you would never have become a true ninja, and you would have never been able to rescue me.' Yamochi put his arm around Mindy.

'What are *you* going to do now, my beautiful daughter?'

'I've decided I'm going to get that metal band together, no more excuses. We're going to be called "Death By Armpit".'

'Amazing!' said Molly. 'Finally, another metal head! You wouldn't believe the shit your brother listens to!' Barry turned to Molly.

'Thanks, Mum. I'm not going to be a gardener anymore. It's a mug's game and I think I've finally outgrown it, if you'll pardon the pun. I haven't got a clue what to do next, though. I need to pay back my debt to the Prophecy Allocation Department too! I wonder if they will accept £1 a week?'

Yamochi pointed at his son across the kitchen table.

'You will help me, my son. We still have so much work to do.'

'Since this is sounding like a careers service workshop,' Molly said. 'I want to announce that I'm going to train as a hairdresser and take over downstairs – I hear there's a vacancy. My old ladies need a decent hairdresser, someone they can trust. Someone who isn't going to shag them before bumping them off for an inheritance. I wouldn't do that in a million years... unless we get a punter from Hove coming in!' Molly cackled.

'Ha ha, you haven't changed, Mum. Let's go out and get pissed tonight, Barry!' said Mindy.

'I can't really; I'm a Buddhist now and we have strict precepts around alcohol.'

'Oh come on, you haven't seen me in twenty-five years.'

'Alright just make sure I don't have more than five pints.'

Molly slinked back over to Yamochi and whispered in his ear.

'I hope you aren't going out tonight, dear. I've got a few ninja tricks of my own to show you.'

Yamochi gulped as his eyes widened. He grabbed Molly and gave her a huge smacker on the lips. Standing up, he beckoned the rest of his family towards him and embraced them. The tears streaming down his face collected in the corners of his smile as he spoke.

'This last twenty-five years have been a terrible sacrifice, but now I'm back with you, I swear I'll never ever leave you again.'

'What happens if we get a black ops secret ninja assignment though, Dad?'

'Okay, I swear never to leave you for more than two weeks at a time.'

'But what if—'

Molly kneed Barry hard in the leg. 'Shut your cake-hole, Barry, and go put the kettle on. There's a good boy.'

'Dad, there's just one last thing that's been niggling me. When I left Robbie I wasn't sure if he was dead or not, I just had to get out as quickly as possible. How did you escape without your powers?'

'I realised Robbie must be dying when I could feel my powers starting to return. I waited for the samurai to chase after you and then went to find him. He was lying face down on the staircase. A vile stench filled the building, I could hardly breathe!'

Barry wriggled awkwardly in his seat.

'What happed next?'

'I decided to jump up and down on his head for about five minutes. When his brains started coming out of his nose I turned him around and jumped on his face. When his brains came out of his ears, I thought to myself, *now he must be dead*!'

Everyone around the table stared at Yamoshi in stunned silence for a few seconds before collapsing into fits of laughter.

Once the hilarity had subsided, Barry got up to make an important announcement.

'On the subject bad odours, you will all be pleased to know my IBS symptoms have cleared up since getting back from Japan. I've been taking these herbs that are working wonders.'

'Hurray!' Everyone cheered in ecstatic unison.

'Thank god for that.' said Molly. 'Mindy's got to share a room with you. Now for fuck's sake go and put that kettle on.'

ABOUT THE AUTHOR

You got to the end...or is it the beginning? I hope you enjoyed it, and I would like to thank you for the opportunity to entertain you with the odd things that live in my head. I am getting help.

If you enjoyed the book, it would be amazing if you could leave a review for me on your platform of choice. It's very easy to get lost in the book swamp and the amount of positive reviews the book has affects how visible it is. This helps me cut down on eating out of my neighbour's dustbin and continue with my writing adventure. Thanks in advance if you do, it means the world.

If you would like the first chapter of the second book in Prophecy Allocation Series **'Hot Love Inferno'** which sees Barry come up against an even deadlier foe. A woman. I warmly invite you to join my Readers List:
nickyblue.com/freebie

HOT LOVE INFERNO

If you are simply gagging to get stuck into book two in the series. You can pick up 'Hot Love Inferno' now at your nearest online bookstore.

In this book the meaning of life is revealed. Kind of.

ALSO BY NICKY

I also write short thrillers under the pen name Mr. Blue that will make your toes curl. You can find my first published story, '*A Watched Pot*' at your at your nearest online bookstore.

Come find me on social media

ACKNOWLEDGMENTS

In no particular order. I owe massive thanks to all of the following beings: **Flo:** Because she's amazing. **Simon Murnau**: Content editing, proof reading, moral filter and brother. **Bobby J**: Ideas and sounding board guru. My comedy muse in human form. **Natalie M Garrett**: Advice, inspiration and faith. **Sam Orams**: Superb photography. **Hannah Moss:** Copy editing **Morgen Bailey:** Copy editing. **Ma and Pa Blue:** For encouraging me all the way. And all my lovely friends for listening to my nonsense. **Beta Readers** Izzy. B, Tracy Hind, Alison G. Laura Fallace, Sian Wilmer, Hai Lun Mitchell, Claire & Tash, Samantha Day. **You all gave me very valuable feedback.**